THE MAGIC CHRISTMAS PINECONE

By E.L. Ferriter Jr.

For Regina and Mike, who always believed in the magic

of fairy tales.

Table of Contents

Chapter 1

A New Friend

Once upon a time, there was a little boy named Eddie who was the youngest in a family of six. They lived in the rolling hills of New England, where winter comes early and usually brings lots of snow. Eddie was a kind boy but life wasn't easy. You see, Eddie stood out. He had big red curls, bright blue eyes and often teased. Because of this, he was very shy and had no friends.

While everybody of course loves snow, Eddie loved it more than anyone. He loved the dancing snowflakes. He loved the swirling mists. And his absolute favorite thing to do, was to run into the early morning winter fog where tiny ice crystals floated in the air like diamond dust.

Nobody knew Eddie had a secret friend hidden in the place where the mist was thickest. Who was this friend? Why, he was none other than the Great North Wind, and this is their story.

It all started on a cold winter's night. All Eddie's brothers and sisters were upstairs doing their homework but Eddie was too little to have homework, so he had his grandpa all to himself. They sat together by the fire for some winter storytelling.

Eddie's grandpa loved to tell stories about the Great North Wind. His grandpa sometimes exaggerated a little, but Eddie didn't know that.

"The Great North Wind is cruel." Eddie's grandpa spoke in a sharp crackly old-man voice that made all his words sound true.

"He has a heart of ice, and knows nothing of love. He's the demise of many ships at sea and the maker of fierce blizzards. Why, if the Great North Wind were here right now, he'd breathe his cold breath on you and freeze you into a block of ice forever."

"Really?" Eddie gasped.

His grandpa nodded solemnly. "Really, and I know his real name. Hardly anybody knows that, but *I* do."

"What is it, Grandpa?" Eddie's ice-blue eyes were as big as saucers. He wasn't sure that he wanted to know the answer, but his curiosity was overwhelming.

His grandpa looked first one way and then the other, as though he were making sure nobody else could hear. He leaned forward and cupped his hand to the boy's ear. Eddie leaned close to hear the secret.

"His name," the old man whispered, "is… Boreas." Then he leaned back in his chair and gave Eddie a stern look, as if to say *Don't ever tell anyone!*

Eddie thought about that. Was his grandpa making it up, or was it real? He wasn't sure. So, he did what he always did when he wasn't sure about something, which was to ask more questions (an excellent strategy).

"Grandpa, can you tell me more about B-… I mean, about the North Wind?"

If the North Wind really was cruel, maybe Eddie would have to re-think his love for winter. So, he hoped his grandpa was wrong.

The old man looked at him for a long moment and then chuckled.

"I think that's enough about the North Wind for tonight. It's time for you to be in bed, young man."

He got up slowly, as old men do, and reached to take Eddie's small hand in his big wrinkled one. Eddie wanted to hear more stories, but he was an obedient little boy (usually), so he let his grandpa take him upstairs, lovingly tuck him in and turn off the light.

But sleep didn't come easily that night. Eddie dreamed of fierce blizzards, and ships wrecks frozen in icy graves. A sudden sound brought Eddie awake with his heart pounding. It was just the winter wind rattling the glass of his bedroom window as it did every cold night but for some reason, it scared him more than usual. He pulled up the covers and curled into a tiny ball.

After a minute or two, he asked himself, "What am I so afraid of? It's just winter, and I love winter."

His grandpa *couldn't* be right. The North Wind was the kind friend who brought him snow to play in. How could anyone so cruel and terrible make the world so white, peaceful and sparkly? Eddie smiled, thinking of the beautiful snowy world outdoors, and fell into a deep and contented sleep.

The next day, Eddie decided to see whether or not his grandpa was right. He ran into the early morning fog. Right into the middle of a great field surrounded by a deep forest which gathered the mist and made it thick with ice crystals. He drew up his courage and called at the top of his lungs:

"BO-RE-AS!"

There was no reply. Eddie waited a moment and tried again but the fog seemed to swallow his voice.

"He must be somewhere else," Eddie thought. "After all, even a North Wind can't be everywhere at once."

But he didn't know where else to look, and the cold fog was making his nose run. He decided to go home and think about it some more. As he turned toward his house, he muttered half to himself, "I just wanted you to know *I* believe you're good."

Suddenly the fog began to shift. First it billowed around Eddie's feet, then it climbed up and formed a huge face in the mist behind him.

Eddie's turned and his heart went BANG, BANG, BANG, in his chest as he saw the giant face looking down at him.

The face looked like a wise old man, with waves of mist drifting behind him forming his long white hair. He had a long white beard, too. A few snowflakes reflected the blue sky overhead to give him bright blue eyes. The mist-man filled the sky. Eddie felt very, very tiny in front of him.

Nobody moved for a moment. Eddie heard something he thought must be thunder, until he noticed the giant face was taking a deep breath. It sucked in the fog all around him like a huge vacuum. The North Wind paused for just a moment then the giant beard parted again...

"Here it comes," thought Eddie. His grandpa had been right, and the next thing he'd feel was the freezing breath of the North Wind turning him into a block of ice forever. He didn't want to be a block of ice!

There was no place to run so he closed his eyes and braced himself for the impact. But instead of the deadly blast, Eddie heard a soft chiming sound and felt a frosty mist that tickled his face and neck (the only parts of him that weren't covered up by heavy winter clothing). When he opened his eyes and looked down, he saw that his whole body, from the tips of his snow boots to the ends of his mittens to the pom-pom on the top of his hat, was covered with sparkly purple frost.

Eddie was relieved not to be turned into a block of ice. But there was something else, he didn't feel cold. Not even a little. He looked up at Boreas in surprise.

Boreas smiled. *"It's been a very long time since anyone has called to me, let alone a child."* he said in his deep foggy voice.

"My grandpa says you're cruel and bad," said Eddie.

"Not exactly," Boreas replied.

"Are you good, then?" asked Eddie.

"No, not that either. I just…"

There was a pause.

"You're just what?" asked Eddie curiously.

"I just… am," Boreas replied.

Eddie thought about that. "Is your heart really made of ice?"

"Of course," Boreas said, smiling. *"what else would it be made of?"*

Eddie supposed that was true. "But, do you really tip over ships and make blizzards?"

"Sometimes," Boreas admitted. *"but I also give the trees, grass and flowers a long cool rest so they can turn green after I'm gone. I cover the mountains with snow that melts so people have water to drink. But my favorite, is making snow for little boys and girls to play in."*

"So that's what you mean when you say you just… are," said Eddie, nodding.

Boreas smiled hugely in his big frosty beard, glad to find someone who understood and loved him. *"Little boy, I'm going to give you a present."*

Eddie loved presents, and he knew what to say when someone gives you one. "Thank you!" he cried. Then, thinking about it, and knowing that great Winds can't give children teddy bears or footballs or ponies, he asked, "What is it?"

"Every Christmas, when you wake up in the morning, you'll see that I've left you a beautiful blanket of snow."

Eddie couldn't imagine anything better.

They met often after that and talked about everything they knew. Eddie knew a lot about small things, the way the grass grew and the way an ant carried a crumb of cake. Boreas knew about big things, about the colored lights that shimmer at night in the coldest places, and the way a cold cloud and a warm cloud fight to make thunder and lightning. They learned a lot from each other and became close friends.

Boreas enjoyed their friendship and many times he would shape the fog into beautiful scenes showing the places around the world where he went.

"Eddie," Boreas promised, *"I'll show you all the places I make the snow fall, all over the world. the ones with glaciers, and the ones with polar bears. the ones*

where snow only falls once a century, and the ones where snow is always on the ground and it's too cold for anyone to live at all."

Eddie couldn't wait.

One day, Eddie thought of something he'd never thought to ask. "Boreas, is Santa real?"

"Yes," smiled the North Wind. *"St. Nicholas does exist. I gave him a present, too."*

"Like mine?" asked Eddie.

"No but I gave him something else. I made him immortal, so he can go on bringing presents to children forever and ever. And I gave him a spell so his home is hidden and nobody can ever disturb him."

"I didn't know you could do that," Eddie said, his eyes wide.

Boreas smiled and nodded, and the fog swirled. Instead of the big bearded face of his friend, Eddie saw a beautiful village with noble castle as it's crowning jewel. The fog shifted again and he saw a high wall all of ice, with a giant totem pole at one end.

"This is the magic gate," said Boreas. *"someday I hope you will go there."* The image disappeared and his friend's face reappeared.

The idea was a little scary but Eddie liked adventures. Besides, Boreas wanted him to go, so he smiled and nodded.

"To open it, you must stand before the gate, take a handful of snow, throw it into the air and say the magic word."

"Please?" asked Eddie. (His mother had always told him "please" was the magic word.)

Boreas chuckled. *"No, not exactly. the magic word is an ancient name for the south wind. But first you must promise me that you will keep that name as secret as you keep mine."*

"I promise," said Eddie.

Boreas looked at him carefully to make sure Eddie was a good keeper of secrets, then nodded. *"The south wind's name is Moriah."*

Eddie thought that was the most beautiful name he'd ever heard. He thanked Boreas for trusting him, and never doubted the existence of Santa again.

Another day, Eddie asked, "What's your home like? Where do you live? Do you live alone?"

"I live in an ice cave at the top of the highest mountain, near the north pole, far too high and too cold for any human to reach," the Wind replied. He used his trick of shaping the fog to show Eddie what his cave looked like.

It looked big, cold and empty. "Don't you get lonely?" asked Eddie.

"Sometimes." Boreas looked sad for a moment. *"But coming here and talking to you makes me feel better."*

"Oh, good." Eddie was glad to hear that.

"I also enjoy traveling." Boreas said thoughtfully. *"I like visit places and watch them change over time."* He showed Eddie place after place, shaping the fog to show mountains and glaciers, icebergs and frozen waterfalls.

Eddie loved the show. He wanted to visit them when he was a grownup, especially hearing how much Boreas loved those places.

"One other thing makes me feel better," said Boreas. With his breath, he made a little flurry of wind and snow. Eddie saw something round and brown that Boreas's breath blew up into the air, and he caught it in his mittened hands. It was a pinecone.

"A pinecone makes you feel better?" he asked, puzzled. How could a tiny pinecone make the you feel anything?

"The rest of the world hides away when the north wind comes to call," said Boreas. *"While all the other plants sleep under the snow, only the pine tree stays green and makes pinecones full of seeds so there will be more pine trees in the years to come."*

Eddie looked at the little brown pinecone in his hands. He'd never thought of it that way.

"Only the pine tree greets me with life and happiness."

"And me," Eddie pointed out. "I do, too."

For a moment, Boreas looked a little startled. Then he laughed. *"And you, Eddie."*

Years passed, and Eddie grew. His shoulders became broad and strong, and his boots left bigger and bigger prints in the snow. And all the while, he kept the pinecone in the top drawer of his nightstand.

The year he turned eighteen, Eddie went out to greet Boreas as always but something was different and Boreas could feel it.

Boreas, Eddie said. "I wanted to thank you. Because of your friendship, I'm not afraid of the world anymore. I'm off to see all the wonderful places you showed me." He paused for a moment then said. "I'm here to say goodbye, at least for now."

Boreas had known this day might come. Boys become men, and lose the magic of their childhood. With a heavy heart he nodded. Eddie turned and slowly walked away. As he disappeared into the fog, Boreas called out to him. *"Remember me."* His voice echoed, and then the echoes died into the silence. The fog that made Boreas's face began to blur and drift. As is returned to mist, a single icy tear that fell to the snow.

Eddie didn't return for a long time. He was a grown-up now, doing grown-up things. But even grown-ups remember their childhood and its secrets.

Time passed and the North Wind saw no further need to keep the promise he made to the boy. Snow arrived less and less frequently to the small town in time for the holidays. As years passed, all they received were cold windy nights with an occasional ice storm or two.

Chapter 2

A Day on the Falls

Grown-up Eddie was like child Eddie in many ways. He loved to travel, especially to cold places. He visited beautiful snowy mountain ranges, icy rivers with frozen waterfalls, glaciers such a bright shade of blue that it made him smile with joy. He was so happy he decided to try something new. He thought ice climbing would be fun.

Eddie walked into a classroom full of students dressed in sturdy boots and thick sweaters. Two teachers stood at the front of the room, ready to explain the important safety protocols they would needed. Today, they would be climbing a frozen waterfall.

Eddie smiled at the instructors as he sat in the front row. The older of the two cleared his throat.

"Good morning. Today we are going to talk about…"

A big merry laugh interrupted the man. Eddie looked around the room to see who it could be.

Everyone had their notebooks out, their pens at the ready and serious expressions on their faces. Who was causing the ruckus?

In the doorway stood a tall woman, watching something that was happening out in the hallway. She had long curly black hair that fell past her slim waist, and her dark eyes were crinkled up with laughter as she turned to face the room. She looked around at the scowling teacher and clapped her hand over her mouth. "Oops," she said through her fingers.

"As I was saying…" started the man, but then the woman started laughing again. It was so contagious that Eddie found himself starting to chuckle too.

This time, both instructors and Eddie's fellow students *all* glared at her. She cleared her throat and wiped a tear of mirth away from her eye. "Um, excuse me," she said.

Eddie grinned and moved over to make room for the new arrival. He knew he should probably be annoyed about the interruption, but it was hard to be mad at someone with such a happy laugh.

The woman slipped into the space next to Eddie, stretching her long legs into the aisle and tossing her black hair back behind her shoulders. She did her best to look serious, but then giggled again. "Sorry," she said.

"And you are?" Eddie asked, trying to control his own grin.

"Petrou," she said, doing her best to straighten her face into a serious expression like everyone else's. "Sonja Petrou. And you?"

"Eddie O'Darvey. Petrou – doesn't that come from the Greek word for stone?"

"The student gets an A," she smiled. "My parents were Greek, I was borne in Britain."

"And I'm Olav, and this is Yuri," said the older teacher impatiently. "Now, can we get back to work, or should we spend all day on introductions?"

Eddie and Sonja cleared their throats and looked away from each other.

Olav was an older, heavy-set man who looked like the craggy cliffs he taught people to climb. His skin was ruddy from many years spent out in the wind and cold.

Yuri, on the other hand, was no older than Eddie, with thick wavy blond hair and handsome features. Yuri was smiling at Sonja, until Olav glared at him. He quickly looked at the floor, blushing a little but still grinning.

"Everybody is here," Olav said loudly. "Let's get started."

Unfortunately, this class included a lot of dry, boring material. Most of the students were taking careful notes. Eddie watched, Sonja doodling in the margins of her notebook. Occasionally she giggled, which made Olav scowl all the harder.

When the class was finished, all of the students had to pick a climbing buddy. Nobody wanted to buddy with Sonja, but Eddie felt quite at home having her by his side. "Don't worry," she grinned at him as they gathered their things to leave. "I haven't killed anyone yet." As they walked together down the hallway, she asked him more seriously, "What are you doing here? This isn't exactly a dream vacation for most guys."

"You wouldn't believe me if I told you," Eddie replied as he zipped up his thermal climbing suit.

"Try me," she said.

"OK, here goes, I was shown these falls by the North Wind when I was a child, and now I've come to climb them."

Sonja stopped dressing and looked at him to see if he was kidding. When she saw the serious expression on his face, she shook her head and laughed. "Right. Did your friend the North Wind suggest any other places for you to travel?"

"Yes, as a matter of fact." Eddie wasn't too thrilled about being teased.

"Well, you'll have to tell me all about them." She elbowed him playfully.

"Forget it," he replied and snatched up his climbing helmet, wondering if he'd made a bad partner choice.

Sonja realized she'd gone too far. "No, really. I want to hear all about it." She touched his forearm apologetically.

Shrugging, he decided to give her one more chance. "What about you? This isn't most girls' idea of a dream vacation, either."

"Actually, it's always been one of my life dreams," she said seriously. "I love challenges, especially ones that people say girls can't do. And I haven't failed yet." Her eyes glowed with confidence as she tucked her hair up under her helmet.

Eddie supposed he could understand that. As they walked outdoors to where the bus was waiting, she took his arm, and he let her. After all, ice climbing can be a bit scary.

One hour later, everybody piled out of the bus at the foot of the towering falls. The students put on their climbing gear. Two by two, they started up the ice, led by Olav in front and followed by Yuri at the rear. Sonja and Eddie were the last pair in line. "Now, Yuri, you're not staying in the back because of me, are you?" Sonja smiled flirtatiously at the blond instructor, who blushed.

"I just maken sure you back safe," he said with a thick Nordic accent. "You remember, like we say in class." Eddie was impressed that the man didn't even try to flirt back – Sonja was, after all, very pretty.

Sonja shrugged. As she grabbed the rope, she began to parrot what she'd learned. "I yell *FALLING* if I start to slip, I yell *ICE* if I break a chunk free, and I stay away from the right side of the falls. Right, Teacher?"

Yuri nodded and turned to Eddie. "You watch out for her, right?"

"Sure thing, boss," Eddie replied, with a smart salute.

Yuri didn't smile. Eddie felt a little bad. After all, Yuri was just trying to do his job and keep them safe.

Sonja wasn't helping. She snuggled up to Eddie's side and wrapped an arm around him, batting her eyes like a movie star. "Eddie'll protect me from the big, bad, ice falls. Won't you, sweetheart?"

Eddie was starting to understand. Flirting and humor were just the way Sonja operated, and the climb would work better if he played along. He rolled his eyes. "I promise, dear."

Then Sonja started up the wall as though she'd been born in a climbing harness. Eddie and Yuri exchanged surprised looks.

Eddie shrugged and turned to follow her.

The climb went smoothly for a while. They were well past the halfway point when Eddie saw that Sonja's climbing was starting to look a bit shaky. Worse, she was drifting to the right side of the falls.

"Hey, Sweetums," he yelled up at her. "A little too far to the right."

"Oh," her voice drifted down to him. "Okay. This route is just a bit easier. Blast..." he heard her grumbling as she started to change direction.

Then it happened. Sonja buried her climbing axe in the ice and a jet of water caught her full in the face, blinding her and filling her mouth with icy liquid. Instinctively she let go of her axe to cover her face. Without the axe to hold onto, she slipped. Eddie's heart leapt from his chest as he watched Sonja start to fall.

He saw the rope go slack and heard a gasp as Sonja dropped past him. He braced himself and shouted "FALLING!" at the top of his lungs, hoping Yuri would hear him in time.

Yuri looked up, startled. "Oof!" he wheezed as Sonja's full weight hit him from above. Eddie's anchor position held, but the force of the collision jerked some of

Yuri's equipment loose. The equipment fell silently downward as Eddie clung desperately to the wall.

The two of climbers dangled there, like a tangled trapeze act – Eddie still attached, Yuri and Sonja swinging gently back and forth below him. "Sorry, Eddie," she said with a smile. But even life-threatening danger couldn't keep Sonja down for long. She grinned at Yuri. "Didja miss me?"

While Eddie tried to figure out what to say to that, Sonya reached up to grab the rope attached to her waist, so she could at least straighten herself out to dangle right-side-up. But when she tried to wrap her hand around the rope, she gasped with pain and her face twisted. "Owww!"

"You okay?" asked Eddie. The last thing they needed was for one of them to get injured.

"For the most part," she said. Then, still trying to lighten the experience, she grinned, "Aren't we just the cutest pair of tangled-up marionettes?" She looked at her fellow dangler. "Yuri, my love, this is loads of fun, but could you please undo this?"

In the next five minutes, Yuri showed them why he was the teacher and they were the students. In a few careful moves, he got first himself and then Sonya back to the wall and right-side-up, then untangled their ropes. Eddie climbed down to meet them. "I told for you to *watch* her," he snapped, smacking him on the back of the helmet.

Eddie had noticed that Yuri's English got worse whenever he got angry or excited. It seemed best not to reply.

"Yuri, you're hurt," cried Sonja. Eddie looked: sure enough, Yuri's glove was torn, and the back of his hand was badly scraped and bleeding.

Yuri grabbed a cloth from his pocket and wrapped it around his hand. "I be okay," he said with a grimace. "But all my forste aid equipment fall. We go down."

"No," Sonja protested.

Eddie couldn't believe it. "Look at us, Sonja. You're hurt, Yuri's hurt. I don't think we have a choice."

She laughed. "There's always a choice. I've spent my life dreaming of climbing these falls, and I'm not about to quit when I'm this close to the top."

They all looked up. The top was only fifty feet above them.

"Besides, I have my two favorite guys to get me up there. You wouldn't take away a girl's dream, would you?" Behind the flirtatious pout, Eddie saw, Sonja was serious.

Eddie and Yuri looked at each other. Yuri sighed. "Forste aid at the top."

Sonya squealed in happiness. "Oh, Yuri!" She kissed his cheek.

"What am I, chopped liver?" Eddie pouted in mock protest.

"Don't worry, ducky, I haven't forgotten you." Sonya blew him a kiss from her non-injured hand.

Suddenly they heard a loud POP! from the direction of the spraying leak. "That doesn't sound so good," Eddie said. Suddenly nothing seemed funny.

Yuri immediately took charge. "No choice now. You to carry her. Get above leak, *now!*" He quickly snapped off one of Sonya's ice cleats, threw a loop around her foot, and anchored the other end of the rope to Eddie. "*You* lead anchor!" He gave Eddie a shove to start him climbing up the last section of the falls. Sonja fell in behind Eddie, with Yuri underneath her supporting her weight so she could climb one-handed.

Eddie strained upward with all his strength, as he heard the cracks and pops that meant the ice was fracturing around the leak. "FASTER!" he heard Yuri yell from below. "NO LOOK BACK!"

Eddie came up to the leak just in time to see a chunk of ice burst out of the hole. The leak doubled. "Oh, no." he muttered to himself. He could hear Yuri shouting at him, but the sound of the spraying water was too loud for him to make out the words. However, he was pretty sure it meant "move it buddy, we're out of time!"

Once he was past the leak, the climbing was a little easier. He scaled the frozen wall like a mountain goat being chased by a snow leopard. The sound of the fracturing ice was deafening.

Then he heard the huge CRASH, the one that meant that the wall had broken free. He heard Sonja's high-pitched scream. The weight on the ropes hadn't changed, so he knew Yuri and Sonja were still attached, but he didn't dare look back to see if they were okay.

Finally, he pulled his way over the top and collapsed in exhaustion. The waiting climbers urgently began hauling on the ropes to pull Sonja and Yuri up over the edge.

Eddie couldn't see his companions through the forest of legs that separated them. Seconds seemed like hours as the burning in his lungs began to subside.

Then he heard something he'd been afraid he would never hear again: Sonja's big, unmistakable laugh. She sounded happier than he'd ever heard her. "Get out of my way!" he heard her shout.

The crowd parted, and Sonja appeared, a sling around her arm. She plopped in the snow next to him.

"That was bloody brilliant! You're my hero!" She leaned over and gave him a big messy kiss on the mouth.

"I know," Eddie said smugly, sitting up.

She smacked him on the helmet. "Don't let it go to your head."

"What?" Eddie said innocently. The two began to laugh.

By the time their laughter had died down to chuckles, the group was heading back to the bus. Everyone looked tired and a little pale: this had been way too close for comfort. Olav was chewing Yuri out in Norwegian – Yuri had a grim expression on his face. Eddie hoped the blond wouldn't lose his job because of the incident. Eddie looked over to Sonja. "I'll be right back."

He waked up to Olav and said that the accident was all his fault and most importantly, Yuri saved their lives. Olav gave him a studied look and walked away. Eddie and Yuri came over and sat down in the snow next to Sonja.

"Lovely, now I have you both." She put her good arm around Yuri, and Eddie put his arm around her.

"I couldn't have done it without you. You saved my life, you know."

Yuri brightened a little – Eddie had a strong feeling everything was going to be ok. "Yousen did good." He put out his hand and Eddie shook it.

A pair of feet appeared in front of them, and they all looked up. It was the tour photographer.

"Wow, if I'd known the paparazzi were showing up, I'd have put on a little lipstick," grinned Sonja. She tossed her wet straggly hair like a fashion model, and both men snickered. The flash went off just as the snickers turned into out-of-control, we-survived-this, falling-all-over-each-other laughter.

"Thanks, guys. I'll send you a copy," said the photographer as he walked away.

After they caught their breath, Eddie said, "Well, if nothing else, this trip has taught me never to quit." He and Yuri stood up and helped Sonja to her feet.

"That's right," Sonja nodded. "Never quit and never surrender."

"Surrender?" asked Yuri, not understanding what she meant.

"Never surrender when you have the chance to win." Sonya told him. "Never surrender when life tries to steal your dreams." She looked back at the falls with a scowl, like an enemy she'd conquered.

Tactfully, nobody mentioned that she hadn't actually finished the climb herself.

"So, what's the next step in your master plan to take over the world?" Eddie joked.

"Well… I've always wanted to fly."

Eddie tried not to think about Sonja behind the wheel of an airplane. "Really?"

She nodded determinedly. "There just aren't enough woman pilots these days." Then she lifted her nose high in the air and strutted back to the bus, limping only slightly.

Yuri and Eddie looked at each other helplessly and burst into laughter. They ran to catch up with her. Eddie put his arm around her shoulder.

"Why stop there? Why not have your own airline?"

"Hmm. Now that you mention it…" she smiled, putting her free arm around Yuri's waist. "Air travel stinks. It's about time someone did it right."

As Eddie and Yuri began to snicker again, she bumped Yuri with her hip. "You just wait and see!"

"Okay," said Yuri with mock solemnity. "I wait and see."

"And how about you?" Sonja asked Eddie. "What are you going to do next?"

"I'm thinking of a nice relaxing cruise. A very, very safe one. If I hang out with you much longer, I'm likely to turn into an adrenaline junkie."

"You say that like it's a *bad* thing," Sonya said earnestly.

Eddie and Yuri rolled their eyes at each other over Sonja's dark head. The three friends limped onto the bus. The engine roared, and the bus rolled away toward civilization.

That night, Eddie and Sonja sat side-by-side in front of a crackling fire in Eddie's hotel room.

"Can I share something with you?" Sonya whispered as she faced the soft flicker light. Eddie looked over and nodded in reply.

"When I was little, I would follow all the boys around and try to be part of the group. When I tried to do all the things they did, they made fun of me and said I was a silly girl and to go away." I don't know which hurt more, being made fun of or having no-one who believed in me.

Eddie looked into the fire. "I know how that feels. I got picked on a lot as a kid. My red hair made it easy. I only had one real friend and no-one believed in him either.

There was a moment of silence as they gazed at the fire and something passed between them. For the first time, Eddie felt he'd met someone he could feel close to.

He looked over at her and said in a soft voice,

" Well, I believe in you. If you put your mind to it, I think you could do anything. I think you're magnificent."

Eddie put his arm around Sonja. She looked over with tears in her eyes. They leaned close. Their lips meet…

Chapter 3

Bon Voyage

After the waterfall adventure Eddie felt like something a bit more mundane. He booked a voyage to Alaska.

The first thing he unpacked after his passport was Boreas's pinecone. It looked a little older and more battered than it had all those years ago, but Eddie never went anywhere without it. He carefully placed it in the drawer of the nightstand.

On the third morning at sea, he was carefully balancing a full cup of coffee as he strolled down the ship's long carpeted passageway. As he reached out to push open a swinging door, someone on the other side pushed it back at him. Coffee exploded all over his jacket.

Eddie was so busy trying to brush off the hot coffee that he hardly heard a voice saying, "Oh, man, I'm so sorry." A hand held out a handkerchief, which he put to good use.

When he looked up, the hanky's owner was standing there, looking embarrassed and nervous. A small, wiry man with wispy blond hair, concerned hazel eyes, well-tailored clothing.

"That's okay," said Eddie politely. "It's washable."

"At least let me pay for the dry cleaning of your jacket," said the stranger.

Eddie shrugged. "Sure, that would be nice. By the way, I'm Eddie O'Darvey."

"Richie Kingsington," said the man, offering a handshake. Eddie wiped his hand on his pant leg and shook.

The small man gasped. "You got a strong grip there, buddy, are you a lumberjack or something?"

"No, but I get that a lot." Eddie was feeling curious about this odd little man. "Seems like you were in a hurry?"

Richie blushed. "I was just trying to get away from the water."

"You chose a strange vacation, then."

Eddie thought this was mild teasing. It seemed to bother his new acquaintance, though. The small man scowled. "My father picked it. He thought it would help me deal with my phobia of cold icy water." He looked away.

"Hey, man, I didn't mean to pry," Eddie said with some embarrassment.

"No problem. It's a family thing. A family business thing."

"Ah," Eddie said, still not understanding. "What's your family business?"

The man looked surprised. "You don't know?"

"Should I?" Eddie didn't want to insult the man.

"I'm *Richard Kingsington.*" Plainly, the name was supposed to mean something.

"Yeah, I got that."

"My dad owns Kingsington Crab and Seafood Company. It's an international household name." Richie sounded a little impatient, as though everyone in the world was supposed to know that.

When Eddie thought about it, he did seem to remember cans of crab and salmon on his mother's kitchen shelves, with labels that said "Kingsington." "I don't cook much," he shrugged. "Sorry."

"Sorry? I'm delighted! Finally, someone who doesn't think I'm just Delmar Kingsington's son." Richie leaned against the bulkhead, looking more relaxed than he had since coming through the door. Eddie smiled, suddenly seeing him as a very likable guy. "Mind if I hang out with you for a while?"

"Sure," Eddie said. "But I have to warn you, I'm on my way out to the deck to watch the ice floes."

Richie went a little pale, but said bravely, "I can handle it."

Eddie wasn't so sure. But, taking Richie at his word, he led the way out onto the deck.

The blueness of the beautifully clear sky was dim compared to the brilliant blue of the glacier. The wall of ice made the ship look like a toy. Down below, a small boat ferried passenger from the ship to the glacier, dropping them onto an icy outcropping where groups could stand to take pictures…

BANG, went something, echoing off the canyon walls. Richie flinched. An automobile-size chunk of ice slid into the sea with a giant splash.

Richie turned his back and stared at the deck.

Eddie paid no attention to him. "Look at those lucky people down there!" he exclaimed. "They must be getting great pictures."

Richie grabbed him by the arm and yanked him around so he could look him in the eye. "You just don't get it, do you?" The small man scowled. "Out there is the very reason I can't take over my dad's business. He thinks I need to get out on the boats to understand the seafood industry, but there's no way you're gonna get me out in that. I'd fight fires if we were a firefighting family, I'd climb skyscrapers if we were a window-washing family. But we're a fishing family, and fish run in icy water. And Richie Kingsington... *does... NOT.*" He was pale and breathing hard.

BANG! went the glacier again. Eddie whirled to watch, grinning like a kid, as another giant chunk dropped with a deafening splash.

"You're not listening to me," Richie gritted.

"Sure I am," Eddie said offhandedly, his eyes glued to the glacier. There was a long pause. Eddie finally realized how rude he was being and turned around to face Richie.

The small man took a deep breath. "So, why are *you* here?"

Eddie decided to tell him the truth. "I'm here because the North Wind showed me this place when I was a boy."

Richie's jaw dropped. "You're kidding."

"Nope," Eddie said cheerfully. "There are places I've always wanted to visit since I was a kid. This is one of them."

Richie shook his head. "And you seemed like such a sane person."

I like this guy, Eddie thought. He wondered if it might be possible to help his new friend get over his fear. He smiled: a plan was forming in his mind.

"I never claimed to be sane," he said. "But at least *I* have the guts to get onto one of those boats and check out the view." He patted Richie on the shoulder, shook his head pityingly, and turned to walk away, toward the small shuttle boats that were dipping up and down in the wavelets far below.

Richie scowled, but did not move to follow him.

Eddie stopped. "Oh, come on, Richie, I dare you! You've made it this far," he coaxed. "Tell you what – if anything bad happens, I'll pay for your whole trip."

Richie's scowl wavered but he didn't move.

"You already found out I'm pretty strong, Richie," Eddie reminded him. "I can handle whatever comes along." Eddie dared a final nudge. "Besides, you wouldn't want to tarnish your famous family name, now would you?"

That did it. Richie marched over, shoved Eddie to one side and began to climb the stairs down to the launch ramp, muttering "stupid jerk thinks he can dare me into getting into the freakin' icy water…" under his breath.

The grumbling continued as the crew members gave them a safety demonstration and made sure they were wearing lifejackets. It continued further as the two men climbed into a boat – which even Eddie had to admit seemed rather small, compared to the hugeness of the freezing ocean all around them.

"Good thing you guys made it down here," said the boatman. "You're the last two of the day. I'll just leave you two on the glacier while I pick up the other guests, then I'll come back for you."

"Perfect!" grinned Eddie. Richie just glared at him. The small man was sitting rigid as a mast pole, at the exact center of the tiny boat.

It was only a few minutes' trip through the icy sea. Eddie and Richie climbed off first, and stood aside so the larger group of people clambered back onto the small vessel.

Richie turned to Eddie. "Ha!" he said triumphantly. "I did it. You satisfied?"

Eddie barely noticed. His eyes were fixed on the great glacier that towered above them like an icy curtain. "Just *look* at that color," he said, transfixed.

Richie's eyes wavered toward the glacier wall for a fraction of a second, then snapped back to the more comforting sight of Eddie. "Yeah, great. It's blue. Now, let's get out of here."

"The boat just left," pointed out Eddie reasonably. "It'll be back soon. C'mon, Richie, take a look at this, it's incredible."

Richie finally gave in and turned to look. His eyes widened at the sight. Then both men jumped as another enormous BANG!, louder than any of the others, shook the ice spur on which they stood.

A chunk of ice the size of a building slid gracefully off the glacier and splashed into the sea, raising a wave of water that was headed straight for them.

"Oh, man, this isn't good," breathed Eddie.

"Ya think?" gasped Richie. "When that hits us, we're dead!"

"Time to think, Rich," Eddie urged him. "Did your dad tell you what to do to survive in icy water?"

Richie was too busy staring in horror at the wave to respond.

Eddie grabbed Richie and shook him. "*Think, Richie!*"

Richie looked at him and his eyes came back into focus. "Curl up into a ball, conserve body heat," he gasped.

"Okay, then," said Eddie briskly. He tightened the straps on Richie's lifejacket, then his own. "Trust me, I'll take care of you," he said, and then the wave was on them.

The force of the freezing water swept them off their feet and yanked Richie's vest out of Eddie's grip. For long moments, he was swirled up and around and down in the icy ocean, like a sock in a washing machine.

He popped to the surface and gasped for air. A moment later, Richie popped up right beside him, gasping and shivering.

However, Eddie didn't feel cold at all. He didn't have time to wonder why – Richie's mouth was open and he was making an awful strangled sound that turned into a thin scream.

"C-c-c-an't breathe!" gasped Richie. "We're d-d-d-ead!"

Luckily, the wave had washed them near the tiny ferryboat, which had already turned around to try to rescue them. Richie, following his father's instructions, was tucked up into a tight ball, bobbing like a cork, buoyed up by his lifejacket. Eddie, warm as toast, swam over and grabbed the orange strap that ran across Richie's back and began towing him toward the ferry. Richie's skin was pale and he had stopped struggling.

As they reached the boat, hands quickly reached down. Eddie pushed Richie up and he was yanked into the boat. More hands reached back down to help Eddie. He felt himself being pulled up over the side and wrapped in dry blankets. When he looked over, Richie was wound up in blankets like a giant cocoon.

Eddie gasped in relief as Richie coughed up salt water. The smaller man's eyes, swollen and puffy, opened just a crack.

Upon arrival, Eddie strolled up the ferry ramp to the deck as though he'd been sunbathing in Hawaii. The giant lump of blankets with Richie peering out of it was carried up by half a dozen crew members and set down in a chair. "Smile!" cried a photographer. Eddie grabbed

Richie by the shoulder with a smile, Richie looked stunned. The flashbulb went off.

"Sorry, not your best look," Eddie said cheerfully, trying to get a smile out of his friend.

Richie's eyes swiveled balefully toward Eddie's as he peered out from his blanket swaddling. Eddie could tell his friend was trying to come up with a devastating reply, but was still too cold and numb to think of one.

Eddie lightly squeezed Richie's damp, blanket-swathed shoulder. "See?" he crowed. "I helped you get over your fear of icy water!"

Richie jumped to his feet, leaving the wet blankets in a tangle on the deck. "That's *it*," he spat, and turned to Eddie, his fists up.

A small man came bustling through the crowd of spectators, shoving the photographer to one side. "Get out of the *way*, idiot!" The new arrival wore an immaculately tailored powder-blue suit and matching tie, but he was red-faced and out of breath. Eddie noticed his carefully styled hair had collapsed and was hanging in sticky strings down his forehead.

Richie dropped his fists and turned to face the newcomer. The red-faced man looked devastated.

"Oh, Mr. Kingsington!" he gasped. "My name is B-b-b-b...Bob Billington, I mean, Billy Bobbington." He stammered.

Eddie looked at the man's shiny name badge and thought the poor guy needed some help.

"Bobby Billings, cruise director," he supplied.

Billings seemed to notice Eddie for the first time. "Yes... thank you," he said shortly. Then he turned back at Richie. "I'm so, so, so s-s-s-sorry for this horrible incident, sir," he apologized breathlessly. "The captain has authorized me to refund the cost of yours and your companion's entire trip, and invite the two of you to join him tonight at the captain's table as honored guests."

At that moment, Eddie began to feel some real respect for Richie. The small man, who a moment before had looked like a particularly miserable drowned rat, drew himself up and squared his shoulders. Suddenly he looked like a member of the royal family, rather than a neurotic rich boy with a water phobia.

"I wonder what would happen if my father heard about this incident," Richie said thoughtfully. "Or the news media." He threw Eddie a sideways wink, almost too quick to see.

Eddie was willing to play along, but he wasn't exactly sure what Richie was trying to accomplish. He decided his best bet was to stay quiet for now.

Beads of sweat had formed along Billings's hairline. The man in the powder-blue suit looked utterly terrified. There was a long moment – several onlookers seemed to be holding their breath.

"Well, I don't suppose we'll need to go that far," Richie said.

Billings exhaled followed by a faint expression of hope.

"We'd be delighted to join the captain tonight," Richie said with a cool smile. "However, considering what we've been through, I believe my friend and I would like…"

Eddie caught his cue. "A better cabin would be nice," he pointed out.

"Your *best* cabin" Richie amended quickly. "*And* another cruise, on your best ship. Someplace to help us recover from this terrible experience."

Billings smiled shakily. "Y-yes, sir, Mr. Kingsington. I, I'll get right on it." He strode away, dabbing at his face with a powder-blue handkerchief.

Richie grinned triumphantly at Eddie, his expression clearly saying, *See, there are things I can do that you can't.*

"Show's over," he said to the bystanders. "You can go now, folks. We're fine."

As the crowd dispersed, he turned to Eddie with a smile. "See? I'm royalty."

"Yeah," said Eddie, rolling his eyes. "C'mon, Prince Charming, or you'll be late for the ball."

As the two strolled away, Eddie asked curiously, "Weren't you being a little tough on our dear cruise director?"

Richie snorted. "You wouldn't say that if you'd heard him making fun of my phobia. Besides, I was going to let him off, until you spoke up."

Eddie laughed. "Well, OK, then. At least that means I followed through on my side of the deal."

"Huh?" Richie looked puzzled.

"I promised I'd pay for your trip if anything went wrong. And I did, didn't I?"

Richie just shook his head and decided to let it pass. "Next time, don't do me any favors."

The two walked on in silence till they came to the elevator. Richie pressed a button, then turned to Eddie with a strange expression on his face. "In the water…"

"Yeah?" Eddie had a feeling he knew what was coming.

"You weren't… cold. You weren't shivering, or anything. Your lips weren't blue. I was about to die, and you looked like you were swimming in the hotel pool." Richie's hazel eyes looked bewildered.

"I guess it was adrenaline," Eddie shrugged.

Richie's eyes narrowed suspiciously. Eddie could see he was working things out.

Eddie decided to change the subject. "C'mon, let's go find out about our new luxury digs." He took Richie by the elbow to start toward the opening elevator door. Richie resisted, clearly about to ask another question, when the ship's photographer came bouncing up to them.

"Hey, guys. Bobby told me to get rid of this picture, but I knew you'd want it."

They looked down at the snapshot: two men, one pale, blue-lipped and trembling, the other pink-faced and healthy-looking.

There was a long pause; suddenly they both burst out laughing.

"Oh, hell," Richie said, finally. "Never mind. Let's get our new rooms."

Chapter 4

The Promise

It had been quite a few years since Eddie had been home and Christmas was coming. He quickly booked a ticket to be with his family.

On Christmas Eve, sitting by the fire, surrounded by his nieces and nephews, Eddie spun stories about all the wonderful places he'd visited. The children were full of questions, but it was getting late and time for bed. All of the children but one stood up to get ready for bed. It was the oldest nephew, Andrew, who stayed in his chair, looking stubborn.

"Is something wrong, Andrew?" asked Eddie.

Andrew hesitated, then blurted, "Uncle Eddie, is Santa real?" Quietly, all the children sat back down, ready to hear his answer.

Eddie didn't hesitate. "Of course, he is! I've seen his home. The North Wind showed it to me."

"The North Wind?" The children exclaimed.

"Yes," Eddie said. "He's my friend."

Well, nobody was going to go to bed after hearing *that* – so, even though it was getting late, Eddie shared the story of his friendship with Boreas. He told the children everything he knew about Santa's home, and the secret gate made from a great wall of ice. He even got out the pinecone Boreas had given him, and let them touch it. But he kept his promise and did not tell them the South Wind's secret name.

By the time he was finished answering their questions, it was very late, and the fire was a pile of glowing embers. "Okay, everybody, it's bedtime." Eddie announced, shooing all the kids up the stairs.

But when he turned around, Andrew was still sitting there, his blond hair turned to bronze by the dim flickering light. "Why don't we get snow for Christmas anymore?" the oldest nephew asked.

"You don't?" asked Eddie, surprised. "There hasn't been any snowstorms this year?"

"None this year, none last year, none for a long time," Andrew said gloomily. "Don't suppose you could ask your buddy the North Wind to bring them back?"

Eddie pretended he couldn't hear the doubt in his nephew's voice. "Hmm, guess you're right. I'll take care of it first thing in the morning." He gave his nephew a reassuring smile and sent him off to bed.

Christmas dawned clear and snowless but Boreas was nowhere to be found. This puzzled Eddie at first, but then he remembered: Boreas only came when there was fog to help him take form. Nevertheless, Santa had come and all the children were happily opening their gifts. Later that morning, when the hubbub had died down, Andrew asked, "So, what about my snow?"

"No fog," Eddie shrugged. "Boreas can't come when the sky is bright."

"Yeah, right," said Andrew, looking away.

Eddie sighed at the sight of his nephew's sadness. "C'mon, let's talk."

The two sat down together on the stairs. "It is too late for me to do anything this year, but I promise – by next Christmas, I'll bring snow."

Andrew smiled in spite of himself. "Really? Cross your heart?"

Eddie crossed his heart and looked over Andrew's shoulder.

"Now don't you think you've been away from your presents a bit too long?"

"Presents!" Andrew gasped, and dashed away.

Eddie could hear his mother's familiar steps as she came over to join him on the staircase. She was drying her hands with a dishtowel and there was a smear of flour on her apron. "So, how are you planning to follow through on your promise to that boy?"

"Mom, it's just a story," he said, blushing.

"I didn't bring you up to be the kind of person who breaks children's hearts," she said. "You know you're his favorite uncle? He looks up to you."

Eddie didn't know what to say. Part of him still believed in Boreas, but it had been such a long time…

"Well, I'm sure you'll come up with a solution," she imposed. "Right?"

"Yes, ma'am," he replied meekly.

"Good." She went back to the kitchen. A few minutes later, he heard her call, "Dinnertime!" and the house exploded with the noise of dozens of feet pounding toward the rich smells coming from the kitchen.

Eddie just sat there and thought. How was he going to fulfill his promise?

"Well, I guess there's only one thing to do," he said to himself. After a moment, he stood up and went to join the others for dinner.

Chapter 5

The Snow BEAR

"I almost didn't recognize you with the beard!" Sonja squealed, after releasing Eddie from a rib-crushing hug. She kissed him on the cheek and then made a face. "Ooh, you're all *furry*."

"So, what do you think?" Eddie asked, displaying his pearly whites through a thick red beard.

"Hmm, not sure," she frowned. "I guess I can always shave it off while you're asleep." The frown dissolved into one of her big laughs. She took him by the hand and pulled him through the airline terminal like an eager child.

They came to a halt in front of a large poster. She struck a pose, shoulders back, smiling her wide celebrity smile, in imitation of the poster. Featured a big picture of Sonja in a business suit. The sky around her filled with airplanes and a headline reading,

"THE FACE THAT LAUNCHED A THOUSAND SHIPS – FLY PETROU AIRLINES!"

"So that's your next career move – Helen of Troy?"

"Hey, it beats paying for a *real* model," she grinned, tossing her dark curls. Eddie smiled, realizing how much he'd missed her playfulness.

"You marry rich or something?" he teased, knowing quite well the reaction he'd get.

Sure enough, Sonja smacked him on the arm. "Hey, I did this all myself! And…"

"… and I'm sure you're never going to let me forget it, either." Eddie loved to tease Sonja.

"Not a chance," she grinned. Eddie felt like he'd known this woman forever. Together, they walked to an airport café.

"But enough about me," Sonja said earnestly as they settled into a corner table. "Your message said you needed my help. What gives, love?"

"I need to get to the North Pole. Or at least, as close to it as you can take me."

"That North Wind thing again?" Sonja narrowed her big dark eyes.

"Well, you *did* ask," Eddie shrugged. He knew Sonja would help if she could, even if she did think he was a little bit nuts.

"Your timing's pretty good, actually," she said. "I may be able to help you out. *If* you can keep up with the big girls."

Eddie raised an eyebrow quizzically.

"I'm entered in the Snow Bowl European Air Race – otherwise known as the Snow BEAR. It's an air race from London to Moscow – which means it ends pretty close to the North Pole. You interested?"

"I'm not gonna be strapped to the wing, or anything, am I?" He wasn't sure he'd put it past her.

She burst out laughing. "Come on, love, I'm not *that* bad." But then her mouth straightened. "However, there is a risk…"

Eddie played right into it. "Don't tell me. You don't know how to fly a plane, right?"

She replied with the best jest of a careless expression.

"Come on, Sonja. You should know by now that nothing you can do will shock me."

"Well, there's just one tiny detail. It's an antique air race." Her eyes searched his face for a negative reaction, and got none. "So, let's just say this plane won't exactly have a lot of creature comforts. It's going be cold, and it might be dangerous."

He set down his coffee and looked her in the eye. "Does it fly?"

"No, I thought we'd just pose for pictures in front of it," she said, very seriously. Then she grinned and reached across the table to smack his arm again. "It doesn't just fly. It's going to *win*. So, are you in?"

"You forgot the helpless smile. You know I'm always a sucker for the helpless smile," he teased.

"Here." She did her best to imitate a timid smile, but she couldn't hold it for long before her big, confident grin took over.

"I'm putty in your hands," he told her. They left the coffee shop together, arm-in-arm.

The next morning, Eddie and Sonja went down to prepare the plane for the race. As they opened the hangar doors, Eddie got his first look at the tiny aircraft, a two-seater with the pilot seated in front and a passenger just behind. It was no bigger than a compact car, with a single fixed wing on the bottom and a propeller on its nose. It looked more like a toy than a plane, especially with its bright yellow paint job.

"So, what do you think?" Sonja was obviously proud of her baby. She began walking around it, checking it carefully to make sure it was in prime condition.

"Looks more like an amusement park ride than a plane," Eddie remarked skeptically. "You checking to make sure nothing's fallen off?"

Sonja came around the plane and shot him a dirty look. She was wearing a leather flight jacket, high black leather boots and tight-fitting pants – she looked sensational and Eddie couldn't take his eyes off her.

She reached down and pulled out the chocks that held the wheels in place. "She's my pride and joy. I had this rose painted onto her side to remind me to stop and smell the roses of victory once they arrive." She climbed onto the base of the wing and pointed to a dainty red rosebud right below the pilot's seat.

Eddie rolled his eyes. Sonja's confidence could sometimes get a little tiresome.

"I had a lot of work put into restoring her," Sonja said.

"And a lot of hours learning how to fly her, right?"

"I never said I knew how to fly, did I?"

Chuckling, she climbed into her seat with a smug grin, tucking her hair into an old-fashioned fur-lined leather helmet and lowering a pair of goggles over her dark eyes. "C'mon, big boy, it's time to go."

Eddie climbed up into the passenger seat and began putting on the similar helmet he found there. "So, where's the classic white silk scarf to complete the look?"

Sonja smiled. "Maybe I'm waiting for the right guy to get me one."

Once he had his helmet on, Sonja turned to face him, her expression more serious than he'd ever seen before. "Right, then. Don't touch any of the controls around your seat. Do you understand?"

Eddie wouldn't have dreamed of it. "No problem."

"And make sure your seatbelt is on good and tight."

"Check, Captain." He saluted her.

She smirked. "I had a glass canopy and heater added to keep us from freezing, but it's still not going to be exactly tropical back there. Your helmet is wired so you can talk to me if you need to."

They closed the canopy and she turned the ignition. Eddie heard a hum as the front propeller began to turn, then the engine roared to life. They rolled out of the hangar, and taxied toward the starting line. Suddenly, a blue plane with a yellow Viking-head insignia cut across their path. Eddie shook a fist at them. "Hey, watch it, buddy!" He noticed the pilots of two more identically painted planes glaring at him. "I was just about to say I liked their paint job, too," he grumbled.

"Don't you worry sweetie, I'll protect you from the big bad bullies," Sonja teased over his headset.

"You promise?"

She laughed delightedly. "I thought it was the man's job to look out for the ladies."

"But I know you're a woman who likes to take charge, right?"

"Darling," she purred. "Compliments will get you everywhere."

They took their place among the other planes. Eddie was astonished by their variety – every color, shape and size of antique plane imaginable.

The race announcer made a speech they couldn't hear through their helmets. Then his arm came slashing down and they were off.

The take-off was flawless, and, to Eddie's surprise, the little plane flew very smoothly. Sonja was a confident pilot and he was really enjoying the experience.

They flew over cheering crowds in front of Parliament in London, then flew down the Thames before soaring over the English Channel. The little yellow plane was as swift as a swallow and easily overtook almost all the entrants as they sped along.

As they entered Paris, the route looped around the Eiffel Tower as spectators cheered below.

"I feel like a superhero," Eddie laughed. "Look... up in the sky... it's a bird... it's a plane... Oh, wait, it really *is* a plane!" he announced as Sonja shook her head in exasperation.

Off into the European countryside they sped. The scenery was breathtaking.

"I think we have one heck of a lead, don't you?" Eddie asked.

"We're making great time," agreed Sonja. "And I have a little surprise for you – a detour I think you'll enjoy. Didn't you tell me that the North Wind showed you a small town just east of the Black Forest?"

"Yes," Eddie agreed, surprised that she remembered.

"Let's see if you can describe it to me."

"Well, let's see. It's on a river, and it has two castles that face each other. And there's a nearby town that has a cuckoo clock shop with a giant clock hanging by the front door."

"Right, sounds like the Rhine," her voice crackled over his headset. "I'll fly low as we go upriver and we'll see what we find."

The small plane skimmed along the river, darting back and forth as it followed the bends. As they rounded one bend, Eddie began to shout. "This is it! This is it!"

Sonja pulled the plane around and made another pass.

"See!" Eddie announced excitedly. "The giant cuckoo clock!" He tapped on the glass canopy to show her where to look.

Sonja laughed. "Well, I wouldn't have believed it if I hadn't seen it. I guess your story is true."

"I guess *some* people need to see to believe."

"Generally speaking? Well, yes," Sonja agreed.

"What is this place, anyway?"

"The two castles are called the Cat and the Mouse," she told him. "I'll have to bring you back here sometime, but for now, we have a race to…"

WHOOSH!

"What was *that?*" Eddie stammered as a blue flash nearly collided with them.

"Speaking of cat and mouse..." Sonja said in an uncharacteristically flat voice, banking the little plane so fast that Eddie's face was smashed up against the side of the canopy.

He righted himself and tightened his seat belt another notch. "Sonja, what's going on here? What haven't you told me?"

She was struggling to outmaneuver the three identical blue planes that were trying to force her down to the ground, and didn't reply.

Finally, she spoke. "Do you have your seatbelt on?"

"Yes, of course."

"Good!" The plane plummeted into a power dive, followed by a loop-the-loop.

Eddie lost all sense of up or down as Sonja ran the tiny plane through a series of corkscrew barrel rolls. His stomach was in his throat and he didn't dare open his mouth to scream.

Then they flew straight up into a cloudbank and headed, as far as he could tell, due south. "Okay," she said after a few minutes. "I think we lost them for now."

"Now can you tell me what's going on?" Eddie was doing his best not to sound hysterical, but it wasn't easy.

Sonja hesitated for a moment, then spoke. "There's another airline that's been trying to buy me out."

"Without success, of course." Eddie knew his friend that well.

"Of course. But now they're getting desperate. My airline's been getting more popular and they know it, so they want to stamp me out."

"Great," Eddie grumbled. "Think you could have told me this a bit earlier?"

Sonja made a face. "They've invested a lot of money in this race, and let's just say they can't afford to lose. Sorry, love, but I needed someone I trusted, someone to watch my back."

There was an uncomfortable silence.

"You may think I'm the crazy one," Eddie said coolly. "But I wouldn't take *you* into harm's way just to win a race."

"It's just that… I needed this." Sonja sounded guilty. It wasn't a good sound for her.

"I thought I knew you."

"Oh, rubbish," she scoffed. Of course, you do."

There was another uncomfortable lull, filled only with the purring of the tiny plane's engine.

"I don't think I can do this," Eddie said.

"Fine," she snapped. "I'll drop you off when we land in Prague. Now let's get out of these clouds, we can't hide in them forever."

"Speak for yourself," Eddie snarled. "My stomach is still recovering from your *last* maneuver."

She huffed. "You know why pilots don't like clouds?"

He didn't answer.

She answered for him. "Because the silver lining around them is usually another plane coming from the other direction. Also, mountains like to hide in them."

Eddie wasn't over his mad yet. "Very funny."

They dropped out of the clouds and the three blue planes were on them again. "Hang onto your knickers!" yelled Sonja, and Eddie felt his teeth grate against each other as the plane zoomed into another power drive, straight down toward the trees below.

Eddie tried to scream "stop," but all that came out was "STAAAAAHHHHH!..." as he felt his cheeks stretching back to his ears.

"You wanted to see the Black Forest? Now you're seeing it up close." Sonja pulled up the nose of the plane and leveled them out just a couple of feet above the treetops. The force of the maneuver slammed Eddie down into his seat.

Sonja let out a laugh that sounded so crazy it made the hair on Eddie's neck stand up.

"OOOOOORIGHT!!! EEEEYAAALEFT!!! UUUUPPPP!" he screamed, near panic.

Sonja's voice barked authoritatively over his headset. "I'll do the flying, love. You watch our six o'clock and tell me if we lose any of them."

Eddie figured the view looking back would be far less alarming than the snow-covered treetops inches from the windscreen, so he turned around, only to discover his hysteria had steamed up the entire back canopy. He cleared a patch with his sleeve. Pressing his cheek to the glass, he reported what he saw.

"Looks like all three are still back there. Wow, they're good."

"Hey," Sonja objected. "Whose side…"

"Strike that," Eddie interrupted. "One just clipped a treetop and he's bugging out."

"I like those odds a lot better." Sonja raised the nose and pulled them upward from the trees. They zoomed over a hilltop, and the trees gave way to a patchwork of fields dotted with farmhouses and barns.

A streak of blue flashed in front of them. Eddie yelled and threw his arms in front of his face.

"Yes, that one will do," Sonja mused aloud.

"What?" Eddie didn't like the sound of that.

"Ever heard of barnstorming, love?" She dropped the plane into another dive without waiting for a reply.

"NOOOOooooooo…." Eddie's stomach turned over. The little plane was headed straight for a big barn at the end of a field.

"Are they still back there?"

Eddie still looking back. "Yes, they are, and they're gaining fast."

"Good!"

"Huh?" Eddie turned face front and saw that both front and back doors of the barn were open. The little plane was headed straight for the doorway. "SONJA, NOOOO!"

Sonja let out another of her ominous laughs. Eddie grabbed the bar in front of him and held on for dear life.

Just as they entered the barn, Sonja gunned the engine. The little plane roared and a cloud of straw billowed into the air behind them, filling the barn with a storm of tan stalks. They shot out the other end like a rocket.

Sonja banked to the side to take a quick look back. The first blue plane didn't make it through the barn, but its pilot did – he shot out the back door like a cannonball, and flew into a nearby snow bank.

"See, that's what happens when you don't wear your seatbelt!" Sonja's laugh returned to its usual glow.

The other pilot saw what had happened and banked upward from the barn. However, the blue plane took out a weathervane and some roof shingles before it turned and flew away.

"How's *that* for flying?!" The crackle of the headphones didn't conceal the triumph in Sonja's voice.

All Eddie could muster was, "You're the Devil."

"I believe that's *She-Devil,* if you please," she said happily.

The little plane changed direction to rejoin the race, speeding across the countryside and then into some mountains. These mountains were huge, and clouds clung to their sides like long sheets of fluffy cloth.

"Don't the girls look beautiful today in their long white dresses?" murmured Sonja.

Eddie, still seething over the barnstorming trick, was silent.

"Well, if that doesn't impress you, maybe this will." Sonja banked the plane around a big cloud formation. Suddenly a huge peak filled Eddie's range of vision. Snow blew softly off its tip, and a giant cloud clung to one side like a billowing sail.

Eddie couldn't help himself. "Wow…"

"Let me introduce you to the Matterhorn," Sonja said, as proudly as if she'd built the mountain herself. "I knew it'd lift your spirits. It's the southernmost point in the race, and it looks like we're the first to arrive. It's also one of the places the North Wind showed you, isn't it?"

"Yes," breathed Eddie, awed by the view. "Right down to the giant cloud billowing off the side."

"It's times like this I forget all about competing and winning," Sonja admitted.

"You mean you *can* think of something besides winning?" Eddie asked.

"Of course, I can." Sonja didn't sound too sure, though. "As a matter of fact, I think it's time I showed you one of *my* favorite places, which just happens to be right along the way. We've got a pretty strong lead, so let's take a minute and do some sightseeing."

"OK," Eddie said. He didn't really believe that anything could outrank Sonja's competitive urges, but he was curious.

The plane banked north once again. After a short while, they were flying over mixed terrain, meadows and forests interspersed with craggy mountains.

They popped around a corner and there it was, perched on a mountainside: a beautiful white castle, a fairyland creation of turrets and spires.

"Is this what I think it is?" gasped Eddie.

"It has a lot of names," replied Sonja. "But I prefer to call it the Swan Castle." She swung the plane into a loop around it.

"After the Swan Lake ballet, right?"

"Very good. The home of King Ludwig the Second."

"Now, there's someone who knew how to dream," Eddie said admiringly. "So, why is this place so special to you?"

"I want to get married here someday." Sonja's voice was softer than Eddie had ever heard it. At that moment, a ray of sunlight broke through the clouds and lit up the front of the castle. The new fallen snow covering the entrance and surrounding forest sparkled in the sun.

There was an awkward pause.

"Well, it's not like I didn't offer," Eddie pointed out.

"You're not going to start that again," scoffed Sonja. "We were just kids. You know as well as I do, that we'd never have been able to achieve our dreams if I'd said yes."

"Yeah, right." Eddie wasn't convinced.

They finished their loop and headed northeast. Eddie was thinking hard.

As the little plane whirred through the sky, he asked, "So, you're trying to tell me that you've changed, and winning isn't everything?"

"Yes," Sonja said. After a pause, she amended. "Maybe."

"I'm not holding my breath." Eddie's flat tone was clearly intended to end the conversation.

Sonja was quiet for a moment. "All right then, back to the race," she said stiffly.

They flew on for quite a while, the silence so uncomfortable that neither was willing to break it. Then the clouds broke and suddenly they saw a large group of antique aircraft flying just below them. "There they are!" exclaimed Sonja. "Looks like we're still in the top ten!" Discomfort forgotten, she gunned her little plane and zoomed toward the other racers.

Once again Sonja proved herself. She easily passed everyone along the way, until at the front of the race, they came upon the two remaining Vikings. The blue planes held the lead, and weren't about to give it up. Every time Sonja tried to get by, they worked in tandem to cut her off. As they entered Prague, Eddie could see Sonja deliberately square her shoulders.

"Sorry, love, but I have to do this..."

"Wha?..." Eddie's breath was taken away by the sudden thrust of the plane shoving him back in his seat.

The little plane screamed up to the Vikings on a wild collision course. Eddie, pretty sure he was going to die in a fiery wreck, was taken by surprise when suddenly the little plane tipped sideways. Perpendicular to the earth below, its wings completely vertical, it slipped between the two blue Vikings!

Sonja let out another wicked cackle. Eddie braced himself for the worst.

Everything went into slow motion as they tipped back to horizontal between the Vikings, yellow wings almost brushing up against blue ones. They were so close that Eddie could see the shocked expression on the right-hand pilot face as he banked away, gaping.

The crowd below cheered wildly as the small yellow plane bulleted through the checkpoint banners, with the other Viking at its side.

Eddie was still shaking as they taxied to a stop. Sonja cut the engines and turned around, her cheeks pink with excitement.

"WHAT WAS THAT?!" Eddie bellowed. "That was worse than the falls! Don't tell me. I don't want to hear it. You are a maniac!" He stomped his foot, ripped off his helmet and threw it to the floorboards. "And you call *me* nuts?!"

"What do you mean, what was that?" Sonja looked honestly surprised. "That was some bloody good flying back there! I just saved our skins, if you hadn't noticed."

Eddie muttered something with "Kamikaze" in it.

"The old Eddie would have supported me without question," she barked. She tossed her headgear onto the seat and rose to bow to the crowd.

"I didn't ask to be dragged into your personal death match!" Eddie stormed.

Sonja looked like she'd been slapped. Her eyes narrowed. "You git! What happened to the man I used to know?"

"I've grown up," Eddie snapped. "And a big part of growing up is knowing that *you can die,* and learning not to take stupid risks!"

Sonja wasn't going to back down. She squared off. "If you haven't figured it out, you stupid sod, life *is* risk! If you're not giving it your all, you're not fully living!

The *old* Eddie knew that and I admired him for it! That was the Eddie I trusted with my life!"

"But you never asked me if I trusted *you* with *mine!*" Eddie yelled.

There was a deadly silence. "And that," Sonja gave a calculated pause, "is why I never married you." She turned, snatched something off the dash and jumped out of the plane.

Eddie was furious. He stood up and yelled at the top of his lungs, "GET BACK HERE! I'm not done with you yet!"

Sonja spun to face him. "But *I,* am done with *you!*" She stormed off into the cheering throng. Eddie wasn't sure, but it looked like she might be crying.

Eddie slammed his fist against the top of the yellow plane in frustration. Should he have trusted her? Out of the corner of his eye he saw something fall off the dash and onto the pilot's seat.

Eddie looked at it and his jaw dropped. It was the photo from their day at the ice falls. Wonderingly, he picked it up. On the back was written, "MY HERO."

Sonja's last words echoed in Eddie's head. He leapt from the plane and ran into the crowd. He could see Sonja's dark curls as she got ready to take the stage, alongside the remaining Viking pilot. He fought his way through the tightly packed crowd to the staircase beside the stage. He looked up just as Sonja started speak and... the lights went out.

Chapter 6

Flying the Friendly Skies

Sonja prepped the plane by herself the next morning. As she climbed aboard, she hesitated, glancing into the empty seat behind hers. She settled into her seat, clipped a photo on the dash, took a deep breath, and touched the photo. Brushing a tear from her cheek, she pulled the canopy shut and fired up the engine.

Eddie's morning, on the other hand, was not off to a good start. He awoke to find himself lying on top of a hard metal surface. When he tried to sit up, he couldn't. It took his drowsy brain a moment to put it together: he was tied firmly atop the wing of a Viking plane.

He looked up to see the pilot laughing as he closed the canopy and started the engine. "You've got to be *kidding me!*" Eddie yelled in disbelief. The pilot, wrapping the traditional white silk flyer's scarf around his thick neck, ignored him.

The blue plane and its twin exited the hangar and joined the other racers. Eddie's plane remained at the back, concealing its cargo.

The race started. Eddie decided that he did not approve of the view: blue sky and clouds, and the occasional flash of another plane dropping back as the Viking zoomed into the lead. He couldn't see the ground over the edge of the wing and the spectators on the ground couldn't see him either.

He felt the harsh wind tear across him. It felt like it was pulling the skin away from his face and hands.

Predictably, the other Viking was right behind them, as was Sonja's little yellow plane. Eddie was tied to the right wing and Sonja was holding her position firmly to the left.

As they entered Russia, Eddie knew Sonja would be ready to make her move. It was then that the Vikings tipped their hand.

Eddie felt himself pulled forward as his pilot throttled back and brought the right wing up – bringing

Sonja in full view of the right side of the plane. He could see her mouth dropping open in horror.

Eddie gave her a helpless smile through his frosty beard and wondered what she would do.

Sonja, safe in her little yellow plane, had taken in the situation at a glance. "Bloody fool," she snarled – she wasn't sure whether she meant Eddie or the Viking pilot. She yanked the joystick and the tiny aircraft jumped forward as if someone had kicked it.

The other Viking was overhead and she was zooming underneath it. She cut it too close; her canopy brushed up against his landing gear, shattering the glass and sending shards whirling everywhere. One of them embedded itself in the photo on the dash.

This time, Eddie's words rang in Sonja's head. *"You may think I'm the crazy one, but I wouldn't take you into harm's way just to win a race."* She shook her head and cursed.

Then she re-adjusted her grip on the joystick, and banked away from the finish line.

She looked around sharply for the Viking with Eddie on its wing. It was nearby, flying low over a frozen lake.

Its canopy was open. Its pilot was reaching over, knife in hand, to cut the ropes and send Eddie plummeting to his death.

Sonja caught her breath. She gunned her little engine to its maximum capacity, flying as she'd never flown before. Her little plane screamed with effort as it brought her directly over the rogue Viking. The tiniest error now would mean the end of everyone.

Heart in her throat, she brought her landing gear down aiming for the fuselage but tore into the left wing of the blue plane. The impact jolted the knife from the pilot's hand. The knife, and a couple of bits of the wing, spun glittering toward the earth. The plane tilted off its axis, throwing the end of the pilot's white scarf over his face and temporarily blinding him.

Struggling with the white silk and cursing, the pilot fought to right his plane. But with Eddie's weight on one side, the damaged wing on the other, and Sonja's little yellow craft still attached by its landing gear, control was impossible. Both planes tumbled toward the frozen lake below.

Screaming, Eddie braced himself as well as he could. WHAM!!! The crash sent a huge crack spreading along the ice, but the plane bounced up and away from the impact site.

The little yellow plane broke free, with minimal damage to the landing gear, and landed safely a hundred yards away. The Viking plane was not so lucky. It sputtered, died, and plummeted onto its damaged left wing. The tip snapped away and the broken wing stabbed into the ice like a knife. The remains of the plane slid on its side along the frozen surface, sending up a huge rooster tail of ice chips as it went.

Finally, the blue plane grated to a stop, the ice cracking ominously underneath it. The pilot leaped out and ran without looking back.

Nearly vertical, Eddie was struggling to loosen the ropes that still tied him to the wing, but the knots had been tied too tight and his hands and feet had gone numb. Sonja ran up, pocketknife in hand, and began sawing at them.

"Y-you came back," Eddie said, surprised.

Sonja didn't look up. "Oh, shut it and help me with these ropes."

"But… you didn't win."

"Depends on how you look at it, love." She didn't look at him, but Eddie couldn't help but notice that she was smiling.

"'Enough adventure for you?" He was genuinely curious about her answer.

She looked up briefly and smiled. "Brilliant." Then she lowered her head and cut through the last rope. "But we're not out of the woods yet." She helped him off the wing, and began to run.

"Whaddaya mean?" Eddie grabbed something from the blue plane and stumbled after her as the numbness faded.

"It takes less space to land than it does to take off. Especially if I'm carrying you, and you're not exactly small. Now, come *on!*" Sonja grabbed him by the hand

and half-dragged him to the yellow plane. He was regaining some feeling in his hands and feet, but the pins-and-needles sensation was still painful.

They jumped into their seats, jammed their helmets on, and the engine roared. "We don't have enough space to take off!" cried Sonja.

"Over there!" Eddie pointed to the tree line off to the left. "Hidden inlet, just past those trees!"

Sonja turned and looked at him. "Of course there is." she said, shaking her head. She faced front. "Well, I guess we've got nothing to lose." The little yellow plane rumbled into motion and taxied off to the left.

Sure enough, after a hundred yards or so, the tree line opened to show a beautiful inlet, trees thick with snow, ice gleaming in the sunshine, and a fine mist drifting over everything. Eddie, of course, had seen it before – Boreas had shown it to him. But the inlet Boreas had shown him hadn't included two massive impact sites, their cracks slowly creeping wider!

The plane, mist billowing around its damaged wheels, reached the end of the inlet. Sonja whipped it around in a tight turn and positioned it for take-off.

"Do we have enough room?" asked Eddie.

Sonja didn't hesitate. "Do you trust me?"

"With my life." Eddie handed her the white silk scarf he'd grabbed from the Viking cockpit.

Sonja tossed it around her neck, grinning. "Well, all *right*, then."

"OK, Ace, show me what you can do!" Eddie shouted. He was thrown back against his seat as the plane sped along the frozen inlet.

A hole had appeared under the Viking's mangled blue fuselage. As they sped closer, the plane began to collapse into the icy water. The cracks spread outward, dangerously close to their path.

"Looks like we've run out of runway," Sonja shouted into Eddie's headset.

"Head for the Viking plane. It gives us more room!"

"Now I *know* I've become a bad influence on you!" Sonja turned the plane on a collision course with the Viking hull, which was slowly sinking into the lake.

"Darling, I love the way our romance never gets dull," Eddie teased.

"Are you saying you see a predictable pattern in our relationship?" shouted Sonja.

"Pattern, yes. Predictable? Never," Eddie laughed.

Just as the ice gave way under their wheels, Sonja eased the joystick backward and the plane took to the air. Eddie marveled at her skill.

Suddenly, the wheels gave out a loud clank. The Viking, sinking sideways, had thrown its remaining wing into the air and tagged the bottom of their plane. Sonja shouted "Bloody hell!" as the plane whipped around.

The small craft shuddered and almost went down, but Sonja valiantly pulled it back into a steady climb.

"Wow, that was close! Good job!" Eddie cheered.

"Maybe not that great..." Sonja replied.

"What? That was amazing! We made it, didn't we?"

"I think we're stuffed," Sonja's voice came over the headset. "That sound was the rest of our landing gear."

"If today has proved anything, it's proved that you can land this plane better than anyone. With or without landing gear." It wasn't just encouragement – Eddie was pretty sure it was true. "Definitely better than that guy down there."

"Well, *that's* not saying much," Sonja laughed. They sped off toward the horizon and the finish line.

Much to both of their surprise, they still finished in second place, with a very showy spark filled landing. When the plane came to a smoldering stop, they leapt from the aircraft and into each other's arms.

Both of them were laughing in delight as Eddie swept Sonja up in his arms and spun her around, her white silk scarf billowing in the breeze.

As they stopped spinning, Eddie looked down at Sonja. She was gazing up at him, her cheeks rosy from the cold and her eyes sparkling with excitement.

"Marry me," he said.

Her eyes glistened. "Yes, darling, absolutely. Of course I will."

Then his mouth was on hers. It felt as if the kiss went on forever.

When they opened theirr eyes at last, he set her down and they walked hand-in-hand away from the bright yellow plane, oblivious of the cloud of smoke and the fire crew racing up with extinguishers. Snow fell around them as they walked toward the cheering crowd.

"So, it seems there *is* something in life more important than winning," Eddie gently teased his new fiancée.

She grinned up at him. "Yes, I guess so."

"And what would that be?"

Sonja stopped and faced him. She tilted her chin up as if for another kiss. "I think you know."

"No, tell me," Eddie said confidently.

Her lips were almost on his. Then she rolled her eyes and pulled her head back. "That would be chocolate pudding."

"… pudding?" Eddie was a little put out by getting neither a kiss nor a confession.

"Yes, Darling. It's Ember's favorite treat."

"And who, may I ask, is Ember?" Eddie was still hoping for the "winning isn't everything" speech, but he was beginning to suspect that his unpredictable wife-to-be wasn't going to give in that easily.

Sonja took a wallet out of her hip pocket, flipped it open and handed it to him. It was open to the picture of Sonja, Yuri and Eddie from the day at the falls.

"Yes? Nice picture of us, but..." Eddie was confused.

"The other side, ducks," Sonja gestured.

Eddie flipped the photo over. It was a photo of Sonja hand-in-hand with an adorable little girl of maybe three, whose auburn curls almost obscured big dark eyes.

He gasped. "You're a *mom?* So... this was the other picture on the dash?"

"Why, yes," she nodded.

Another question occurred to Eddie, and it seemed important. "So, who's the daddy? Yuri?"

Her face hardened. "Yuri's blond, you git. Brunette plus blond doesn't make redhead."

Eddie felt dizzy. Suddenly he found himself sitting in the snow, still gazing at the picture with his mouth hanging open.

Sonja plopped down next to him. "So, Daddy – any other questions?"

He had trouble finding his voice. "Why didn't you tell me?"

"Luv, if you haven't noticed, you're not the easiest person to get hold of."

Eddie had to concede the truth of that. He couldn't stop staring at the photo. "Ember… like the glowing embers in the fire, the night after we climbed the falls."

"In the hope that her heart would always stay just as warm," Sonja nodded.

There was a long pause.

"I guess 'sorry' doesn't quite cover it?" Eddie whispered.

"It might," she conceded. "Now that you've come to your senses and trust me for a change."

Eddie didn't reply. He simply got up, pulled her up beside him, put his arms around her waist, lifted her off the ground and kissed her again.

Her arms stole around his neck and she softened against him, happily returning the kiss.

He gently set her down. She looked into his eyes and smiled. "I have someone for you to meet."

"She's here?"

Sonja nodded. "Waiting for us back at the ceremony."

A car pulled up beside them, and they were driven to Red Square to watch the winner's cup being awarded. The minute they stepped out of the vehicle; cheers filled the air.

"What's all the fuss?" wondered Sonja. "After all, we only came in second."

"First," corrected a smiling official. "The Viking team was disqualified – we have footage of the gentleman bound to the wing of their aircraft. Would you like to file criminal charges as well?"

Sonja looked at him questioningly. Eddie shook his head – he was way too happy to care what happened to the Vikings. He took Sonja's hand and they walked toward the winner's platform.

As they approached the crowd, a little red-haired girl broke free from her governess's hand and flew into Sonja's arms. "Mommy!"

Sonja hugged the wriggling child, then turned her so she could look at Eddie. "You know who this is, don't you, poppet?"

"Daddy?" Ember asked wonderingly.

Eddie's eyes filled. "Yes, Ember."

The little girl held out her arms to him. He took her from her mother and held her tight to his chest, feeling happier than he'd ever felt in his life.

The governess came up. "Call for you, Mum." She handed a mobile phone to Sonja, who was watching her daughter and her husband-to-be getting acquainted.

"Mummy says you're going to the North Pole," Ember said excitedly. "Daddy, will you see Santa there?"

"Yes, I hope so," Eddie replied.

"Will you give him my letter?" She pulled a crayon-addressed envelope from her coat pocket and handed it to him. Eddie took it and tucked it carefully away in his breast pocket. "Oooh, thank you, Daddy!" She threw her arms around his neck again.

Sonja rejoined the conversation. "Well, darling, looks like you have another very important reason to continue your trip."

Eddie smiled and patted his pocket.

"As for me," Sonja continued, "it looks like I'm stuck for a while. Viking Airways just filed for bankruptcy. It seems they were counting on their winnings to keep them going. I need to get back to London to buy them out."

Eddie's face fell.

Sonja looked sympathetic. "It'll only be a few weeks, love. I'm going to put you on the Trans-Siberian Railroad. That'll take you as far north as Murmansk."

"And then?" Eddie asked.

"Dunno. You're clever, you'll figure it out," Sonya said blithely.

"Wait a minute – I think I have an idea. Give me your phone." Eddie held out his hand. I'm going to call a good friend.

Sonja gave him the phone. Eddie dialed a quick sequence and hit the speaker button. "Hey, Rich, guess who this is?"

"Eddie?" the voice crackled over the long-distance line. "You jerk! Where the heck have you been?"

"Tell you later," Eddie promised. "Right now, I need your help. You got any ships in Murmansk? I need a lift back to the States, with a slight side trip."

"You're in *Russia?*" Richie sounded incredulous.

"Moscow, to be precise."

"This isn't another of your wild adventures, is it? 'Cause if it is, count me out!"

Sonja looked skeptical. "You sure this is your best mate?" she whispered

Eddie grinned and sent her a thumbs-up sign. "Now, Richie, you know you're my best bud. I wouldn't do that to you. Besides, you haven't answered my question."

Richie grumbled. "No ships there. I have one in Tokyo, though."

"Tokyo?" Eddie couldn't see the logic of that.

"It's the oldest in the fleet and ready for retirement," Richie explained.

"I was going to take it back in the spring, but I guess I could make an exception and sail it back now. But you'll have to work as part of the crew – she's a working ship and we don't have room for passengers."

Eddie wasn't sure what Richie was up to, but being crew on a fishing ship actually sounded like fun. "Sure, why not?"

"Good, because I'm going to be your captain. Get ready to work your butt off." Richie actually sounded more certain than Eddie had ever heard him sound before. Apparently being a captain agreed with him.

"I-I Captain." Eddie assured him.

"Good. Meet us at the Tokyo dockyards, Pier 7, in three weeks. Got it?"

"Um, sure," Eddie said. Things seemed to be happening awfully fast. He handed the phone back to Sonja, his head spinning.

"Tokyo?" Sonja queried, looking almost as confused as Eddie felt. "In case you hadn't noticed, love, Tokyo's the wrong way."

"It'll get me farther north, eventually," he said, hoping he was right.

She shook her head. "Unpredictable – I really said it, didn't I? Well, good thing the Trans-Siberian runs east."

"Now for more important matters." Sonja continued.

She took his arm and raised her head proudly.

"Let's go get my prize money."

The trio walked into the cheering crowd full of flashing cameras.

Chapter 7

The Hercules

Mount Fuji covered in snow was a stunning sight to behold.

"Wow, this is it," Eddie breathed. "Just like Boreas showed me." He'd expected to feel triumphant. After all, he was nearing the end of the quest on which his friendship with the North Wind had launched him all those years ago. However, he didn't. It felt, well, bitter sweet. He wished this trip were over and he could get home to his fiancée and daughter. The feeling stayed with him until the train arrived in Tokyo.

Well, there was nothing for it. He shook off the odd feeling and headed for the docks, tossing a duffel bag containing some sturdy clothes and the North Wind's pinecone – over his shoulder.

Richie and his crew were waiting for him when he arrived. "Permission to come aboard, captain?" he shouted from the foot of the gangplank.

Richie looked at him. "I don't know about that, greenhorn." He turned to face his crew, a ragtag bunch wearing every kind of clothing imaginable. "Whaddaya think, boys – should we take him?"

"Dude," said a gangly crew member. "Ain't you that airplane guy from the news?"

"Yeah," another one laughed. "Mr. Celebrity wants to see if he can cut it at sea."

Everyone had a good laugh at Eddie's expense, while he stood there and grimaced. "Maybe. As long as he pulls his own weight," an older crew member growled.

Richie let the teasing go on for a while before he broke character and began to laugh. With a big welcoming smile, he stuck out his hand and pulled Eddie aboard.

The voyage went on for weeks and Eddie got a first-class education on baiting crab pots. He was filling in as ship's cook as well. He wasn't a very good cook, but men who work all day out at sea aren't usually too picky about their food.

One evening, while Eddie was down in the galley stirring an enormous cauldron of simmering soup, the intercom squawked to life. It was Richie.

"Hey, Swabby, (Richie's new nickname him.) what's for dinner?"

Eddie flicked the intercom switch as he mopped sweat from his face with the hand towel he kept in his back pocket. "My famous seafood soup, sir," he said cheerfully.

A chorus of grumbles exploded from the intercom as the crew expressed their opinion of his cooking. "Come on, guys. It's not *that* bad," he grinned, drying his hands with the towel.

More grumbling, with Richie cutting it off in the middle. "Take a break and come up on the bridge for a minute. I got something to show you."

Eddie put a lid on the boiling pot and secured it to the stove. As he ascended the stairs onto the bridge, he saw Richie holding the wheel, staring intensely out the window.

"What are you looking at?" he asked.

Richie's gaze never wavered. "Check this out. I've never seen fog like this before. It's full of floating ice crystals."

"I have," Eddie said quietly, his heart pounding wildly in his chest.

"I'm glad you're happy, because I can't see a thing." Richie looked frustrated.

"Is there supposed to be anything out there?"

"Radar says no. This late in the season, everything's frozen down."

The radar screen, as if in protest, blacked out. Richie turned and smacked the side of the wooden case and the screen flickered back to life. "What a hunk of junk," he said in annoyance. "I have a whole fleet of ships, and we're still sailing this old relic."

"I thought you liked this ship," Eddie said in surprise.

"Of course I do, I grew up on the Hercules." Richie sounded a bit annoyed.

"You mean, you grew up on him whenever he was in port," Eddie corrected.

"Let's say it's a love-hate relationship." The radar went out again. Richie pounded on the side of the case like an old man with an out-of-whack TV set. "See what I mean? Do me a favor and head up to the bow for a minute while I get this up and running," he grumbled.

"Sure," Eddie replied.

On the way out, he grabbed a parka from one of the pegs by the door.

He walked down the ice-covered steps to the bow, looking out into the fog. It was just as beautiful as he'd remembered it. He reached into his pocket and held the pinecone hidden there.

"What the heck," he thought. "Let's give it a try." He took a deep breath. "Bor-e-as!!" But the twisting fog seemed to swallow up his voice.

He looked over his shoulder at Richie, who was banging away at the radar case. Shrugging, he tried again, much louder. "BO-RE-AS!!!"

He waited. Still nothing.

Eddie looked down and sighed in disappointment. He turned to head back to the bridge.

Out of the corner of his eye, he saw something forming in the fog. His heart leapt in his chest as he saw the face of his old friend the North Wind. But then the fog shifted again. The friendly familiar face shimmered and changed into the leading edge of an enormous iceberg.

Eddie yelled in alarm and ran for Richie, waving his arms and shouting. Unfortunately, the fog muffled his voice like a nightmare where you scream for help and no sound comes out. He made it to the wheelhouse stairs, where Richie was still fussing with the radar, and screamed "ICEBERG! ICEBERG!!"

Richie looked up and his eyes got huge. He grabbed the throttle and yanked. It was too late.

An enormous crash filled the air. Both men were thrown from their feet by the impact. Eddie thrown backward, toward the ship's bow. As he hit what was left of the railing, a shower of ice chunks ranging from pebble-size to boulder-size descended from the iceberg around him. Eddie hollered again and threw his arms over his head to protect himself.

When he looked up, he saw that Richie had been thrown away from the wheel, and it was spinning freely. The throttle, unattended, had been shoved to full-forward. The shriek of tearing metal filled the air – it sounded as though the ship itself were screaming in pain.

Eddie saw Richie stagger to his feet to seize the wheel again, but it was too late – the forward motion of the iceberg cleaving the ship's bow pulled them over. The Hercules was being dragged onto its port side for another collision.

Eddie braced himself for the second impact. It sounded even worse than the first one.

Looking through the window, he saw Richie cut the engine. The air grew suddenly quiet, except for the distant yells of the crew coming from below. Eddie could see Richie through the window, screaming what looked like "Mayday! Mayday! Collision!" into the radio.

Eddie ran. He used the railings to keep himself from sliding into the icy water as he made his way to the port side.

His worst fears were confirmed: the ship was wedged into the side of the iceberg. The side railing and much of the deck were crushed beyond recognition.

However worst news was the lifeboat. It had taken a one-two punch: first pinned by the monstrous iceberg, then crushed by a huge chunk of ice which had fallen on it.

"Good thing there's another one on the starboard side," Eddie thought.

The crew poured onto the deck, slipping and sliding, trying to scramble into their gear as they ran. Richie popped out of the wheelhouse as he thrust on his parka. "Captain!" a crew member yelled. "We're takin' on water, fast!"

Eddie had never been more impressed with his friend – Richie snapped into emergency mode as if he'd been born barking orders.

"OK, boys," he shouted. "Put on your cold-water survival gear – we're going to abandon ship! I've already sent a mayday and the lifeboats have extra radios. We'll leave as soon as everyone's geared up."

"Captain, the port side lifeboat is toast," Eddie said.

"Fine, we'll take the one on the starboard side," Richie said immediately. The men scattered into frenzied activity.

Somewhat to Eddie's surprise, everyone was geared up and ready to go within moments. But their problems weren't over. Although someone had removed the starboard lifeboat's weather cover, it hadn't moved an inch.

Richie burst through the crowd of men gathered around the lifeboat. "What's going on?!"

"Boat's frozen to the deck, Cap'n," a crew member replied in a panic.

"Grab an axe off the rack!" Rich ordered.

"Aye aye." The man ran to obey.

Someone shouted and pointed. Everybody followed his pointing finger.

"You've got to be kidding me!" Richie said in disbelief.

But there it was – another giant iceberg, headed their way. "Unbelievable," someone muttered.

The axe arrived, and men began taking turns hacking away at the frozen deck clamps. Others had seized the edge of the lifeboat and were trying to rock it free. Still others were shouting excitedly as the second iceberg loomed closer and closer. Richie was shouting orders, trying to keep everybody focused.

Eddie grabbed him by the shoulder. "Come with me to the galley," he said with a determined gaze.

Richie looked at him like was out of his mind. "In case you hadn't noticed, I don't think it's dinner!"

"Trust me," said Eddie. "I have an idea."

Richie looked at him for a long moment, then turned to the men and shouted, "Keep at it, boys! Swabby and I will be right back! If you break it free, don't wait for us!"

The two men ran.

The galley was a mess, with dishes broken and silverware scattered. But the boiling cauldron of soup stood where Eddie had left it, anchored to the stove and firmly lidded.

Eddie grabbed a couple of oven mitts and threw them at Richie, then donned a pair himself.

Richie got the idea. A huge smile spread across his face. "At least this horrible muck will be good for something," he said.

The two men carried the heavy, steaming pot up the deck.

The crew was still wildly chopping at the iced-over clamps with what was left of the axe. Captain Rich yelled "Watch your feet, boys!" and they dumped the steaming pot.

The boiling soup flooded over the deck clamps, creating a huge cloud of steam that rose up around it. The crew, catching on, redoubled their efforts to rock the boat loose. With a mighty "crack," they succeeded – the boat came free!

The iceberg was just yards away – there was no room left for the lifeboat to fall into the water. Working as if they'd rehearsed for weeks, the crew hoisted the small craft onto their shoulders and ran toward the bow. Just as they hoisted it into position over the railing, the iceberg hit with yet another giant crash, sending the life boat sailing out over the open ocean, shedding bits and pieces of supplies and food as it flew.

Richie lunged after the flare gun and flares, but they slid down the deck and disappeared into the depths.

For once, the crew's luck was with them – the boat landed right side up.

"Finally a break," Richie gasped. "Jump for it, boys!"

The Hercules was being crushed like a tube of toothpaste, back to front, and anybody left standing on the deck was going to be crushed along with it.

The crew jumped. Some made it, some didn't. The ones that did, got busy pulling the others out of the water and into the tiny craft. Their cries and splashes were lost in the horrible grating sound of the Hercules being reduced to splintered planks.

Eddie was still on deck. So was Rich, who turned back toward the wheelhouse. Eddie grabbed his friend's shoulder. "Where do you think you're going?"

"I have to get the spare flare gun!"

"You sure?" Eddie remembered his friend's terror of icy water.

"Just get out of my way!" Richie shoved Eddie toward the lifeboat and turned to run, ducking a flying plank. Eddie reached out and grabbed his friend by the back of his parka.

"Man overboard!" he shouted, tossing Rich's flailing body toward the lifeboat below. The captain landed on two of his crew with a thud, and lay immobile.

"Push off," Eddie yelled down to the men below. "I'll catch up!" He ran for the bridge.

Richie twitched groggily and sat up. "EDDIE!" he screamed. "You maniac, get down here!"

"Coming right down!" Eddie shouted in reply, brandishing the red flare bag he'd retrieved.

Then came a blinding flash, accompanied by an earsplitting "BOOM!" Richie and the crew shielded their eyes from its intensity. When they opened them, the air was filled with a shower of pulverized crab chunks.

"EDDIE!" shrieked Richie. His men, thinking fast, grabbed him just as he was about to dive after his friend. He burst into tears.

Silence formed around them, except for the occasional patter of a bit of debris hitting the water and the sound of Richie's sobs. Around him, crew members rubbed their eyes, trying to clear the temporary blindness from the brilliant light of the explosion.

"He was a brave dude, man," one of the crew offered. The boat rocked quietly in the diminishing waves. They sat for what seemed an age amongst the smoldering debris that floated around them…

"What's with all the glum faces? We made it, didn't we? See, I even got the flare gun." Everybody swiveled in unison. There stood Eddie in the back of the lifeboat, looking like a drowned rat but with the dripping red bag clenched in his hand.

"*Whoa*, man," said the gangly guy.

Eddie grinned. "The blast blew me right off the deck. Talk about a close call."

Richie's eyes narrowed. "What the… Wait a minute, why didn't you freeze in the water? It's below zero."

Eddie started to say something, but Rich interrupted him. "Don't tell me. Adrenaline, right?"

Eddie shrugged with a smiled. The crew looked at him blankly. They clearly weren't buying it, but they were too tired and shaken to bother.

Richie cleared his throat.

"Well. Let's get on with it, boys. Break out the radio so we can see who's around for a pickup."

Someone flipped a switch and the radio buzzed to life. Rich grabbed the microphone. "North Point Station, this is Captain Richard Kingsington of the Hercules. Do you read me? Over."

"This is North Point Station. We read you loud and clear, Captain. Over," crackled the reply.

"I have a stranded crew on a lifeboat. I believe we're due east of your location, over," said Rich.

"Roger that. Judging from that flash, you're three miles west of our location. Everyone make it? That was quite a blast. Over."

All eyes went to Eddie. He tried to look unremarkable. Rich cleared his throat again. "Yes, everyone made it. Over."

"Great, you're a quarter mile from the edge of the ice pack. If you can row due north, we can meet you. Over."

"Roger that. Radio us when you're close and we'll send up a flare," said Rich. "Over and out."

"Wait!" said the voice. "We have a local advisory alert."

Chapter 8

A Long March

"An advisory alert?" Rich said disbelievingly. "What else can possibly go wrong? Over."

"We have a dangerous polar bear roaming the area. Be on your guard. Over."

Richie sighed. "Of course. A polar bear. Roger, we'll keep a lookout. Over."

"Over and out," said the voice.

"Great," said Rich, tossing the microphone away in disgust. "Now we have a killer polar bear. What's next – Martians?"

"Now, Rich, the guy said 'dangerous', not 'killer'. Aren't you being a little overdramatic?" Eddie thought his friend might be able to use a bit of perspective at this point.

Rich wasn't having it. "Overdramatic?! Just look at my ship!" he shouted. They all turned. There was no ship left to look at, just a few smoldering piles still floating around them. "I think I speak for all of us when I say *I've had enough adventure for one day!*"

He had a point. Eddie thought.

Rich sighed. "All right, boys. Grab the oars and let's get out of here." The crewmen, who looked a little like they were done with adventure too, picked up the oars without comment and began to row.

Eddie sidled over and plopped down next to Rich. He leaned over and whispered into his friend's ear. "I'm really sorry about your ship."

The friends stared out together at the slushy ocean gently lapping up against the sides of the boat, bits of debris floating, sinking and smoking all around them. A picture frame, its glass cracked and its wooden edge crushed, floated by. Rich reached down to snatch it out of the water and they stared in disbelief.

It was the photo of the two of them, taken after their glacier misadventure.

"You see?" Eddie said softly. "It's all good."

Richie folded the picture and tucked it carefully into his jacket pocket. "It's okay," he said finally.

"I had insurance on the old wreck."

He snickered and jabbed Eddie in the ribs, and the tension was broken. "All right, boys, let's get a move on!" he hollered. "I'm starving, and I'm sure there's a better meal in town than the fish soup we're wearing."

"You got that right!" Eddie shouted. "You guys usually smell pretty bad, but today you've hit an all-time low!" He grinned through his frozen beard.

"Pot, kettle, black." Rich, grinning back at Eddie, held his nose, then cracked up. The crew snickered. (In truth, everybody on the ship had always smelled of sweat, fish bait and diesel.)

"By the way," Eddie said. "Got something for ya." He plopped the soggy red bag in Rich's lap. "Special delivery, air mail."

Rich yelped and jumped to his feet as the freezing water threatened soaked into his trousers. It took him a minute to regain his composure, then he began to laugh along with everyone else.

The little craft cruised silently through the light mist, pulled by the strong backs of the crewmen and their oars. They made it to the edge of the ice pack just in time.

"Okay, everyone – it looks like that fog might come back, so let's head due east and get closer to the rescue party," Rich ordered.

Grabbing a few supplies and a couple of in-case-of-bears oars, they headed east. Richie moved to the front of the group and pulling out his sturdy hand compass.

"Well, aren't you the Boy Scout," Eddie teased, joining him.

"Luck favors the prepared," Rich said with pride. "C'mon, boys!" And off the tiny group marched.

They'd been walking about half an hour when the ice fog returned. Eddie could see dim shapes moving in the fog, so he slowly drifted to the back of the line of trudging crewmen, and paused to let them get a few yards ahead of him.

"Boreas, is that you?" he whispered. "It's me, Eddie. I'm back."

The fog swirled. Had he seen something? He wasn't sure. But he got no response. He trotted back into line. Rich was there waiting for him.

"What do you think you're doing? Eddie, I swear you're always up to something. And I want to know what it is."

Eddie wasn't sure he wanted to talk about this with Rich, much as he loved his friend. He walked faster, hoping to avoid the conversation.

Rich was right on his heels. "I heard you calling out to the North Wind," he whispered, too quietly for the rest of the crew to hear. "Does this have anything to do with that crazy tale you told me when we first met?"

Eddie kept walking.

"Or did that blast just rattle your marbles? The way you're acting, I think you lost a few," Rich insisted.

By this time, they'd moved halfway up the line. Frustrated, Richie grabbed Eddie's shoulder and spun him around. "Are you listening to me? Tell me what's going on!"

"You wouldn't believe me if I told you," Eddie sighed.

"Try me."

Eddie gave up – Richie clearly wasn't going to drop it. "Well…" Then his eyes got huge. "Bear!"

"Bear what?" Richie asked, looking puzzled.

Eddie lifted his arm, pointed back the way they'd come and hollered at the top of his lungs. "BEAR!"

It seemed to Eddie as if the whole scene were happening in slow motion…

The polar bear, annoyed, began to charge…

The crew scattered in panic…

The first man in the bear's way was batted into the air like a rag doll and flew into a snowbank…

Another man swung at the bear with one of the oars, but the beast broke it into splinters with one swat of its massive paw…

Eddie was next in the bear's path. Everything sped up again.

He turned to run, but slipped on the ice and fell on his back. The bear was atop him before he could move, gazing directly into his wide eyes. He could smell the enormous animal's foul breath as it slavered over his face. Its drool dripping on to Eddie's cheek.

Suddenly a flash of blinding light exploded from the bear's shoulder and shot into the sky.

The bear reared up and roared in pain, exposing a broken front tooth, then barreled off into the icy fog.

Eddie rolled off his back and onto all fours, still panting in terror. He looked up to see Richie standing five yards away, a smoking flare gun still shaking in his hands.

"Wow, that was brilliant!" Eddie gasped. "What an adventure!"

Richie didn't lower his arms. The gun still shook in his hands.

Climbing to his feet, Eddie went to his friend and gently lowered the gun toward the ground. "Hey, Buddy, it's okay. He's gone."

"Okay?! OKAY??!!! No, it's NOT OKAY!" Richie screeched, tossing the gun aside. "I've had enough adventure for three lifetimes, thank you very much!" His hysteria continued to build as the crew gathered around, murmuring with worry about their normally stalwart captain.

"Richie, the man says, 'let's go on a trip! Set sail on my ship and watch it get crunched into a pancake by a giant iceberg, and then let's get ambushed by the Abominable Snowbear! Ha! It'll be just like the good old days!"

"Richie," Eddie implored. "You're beginning to freak out the crew. You might want to calm down a little…"

"Calm?" Rich laughed crazily. "Me, calm down? Why, I'm just getting started!" His eyes were wild.

"Dude! Listen!" shouted a crewman. Even Richie knew enough to pipe down at that moment. And, sure enough, a few seconds later they could hear the buzz of snowmobiles drawing closer.

Eddie turned, his hand still on Rich's shoulder. "All right! The cavalry is here! You see, Rich, it's all goo-"

"Don't say it," Richie grumbled. "Don't you dare." His teeth were clenched so tightly Eddie worried they might crack.

Within moments, a group of snowmobiles were by their side. "Everyone all right?" the leader asked as he cut the engine.

"Sure, if you're not counting the crazy people," Richie replied, glaring in Eddie's direction.

The rescue party leader was a heavyset man with a thick brown beard and weathered features. He glanced over at Eddie and decided to ignore Richie's remark. "Well, that's good," he said vaguely. "Here's some fresh parkas and cold-weather gear for the trip back."

They geared up and were off in record time.

Back at the station, they were greeted by a small group of villagers, mostly small dark-skinned people dressed in parkas lined with rich fur. The crew pulled up and dismounted from the rumbling machines.

Eddie removed his headgear and went over to Richie. "Hey, buddy, you okay?" he asked, nervously.

Richie, to his surprise, seemed amazingly calm. "I'm fine now," he said smugly. "We're safely back in something approximating civilization."

The station leader walked over and stuck out his hand to Richie. "Hi, I'm Manny White. You must be the famous Rich Kingsington."

"Yes, that's correct," said Richie, shooting Eddie a sidelong "you see?" glance. Eddie rolled his eyes.

Manny did a double-take. "Wait a minute," he said, staring at Eddie. "Aren't you that guy from the air race?"

"Guilty," Eddie replied, shooting a "neener neener" glance back at Rich, who pretended not to notice.

"Wow," said Manny. "We're honored to have both you and your crew as our guests. We don't often get celebrities like you two in these parts. Let's get you into the main barracks so you can warm up and get a hot meal."

As they walked through the village, the locals stood in small pockets, staring. Eddie waved cheerfully at them. Richie pretended they weren't there. The rest of the crew trailed behind uncertainly.

Manny was still talking. "Room's a bit limited, so you'll need to double up for the night. I'm sure you're used to it…"

"Your windy buddy sunk my ship," Rich whispered irritably to Eddie.

"As I recall, *Captain,* you were the one behind the wheel." Eddie was starting to feel a little peeved himself. Was he supposed to be responsible for everything Boreas might be part of?

"Don't confuse me with the facts! Besides, I don't think you appreciate my fast thinking and…"

They approached the doorway of the main rec-hall. Two figures stood by the door holding hands, both clad in traditional Eskimo garb: an old man and a small boy of about five.

Manny, wisely, interrupted. "I'd like you to meet these gentlemen, fellas. This is Ku-dako, the local shaman or medicine man, and his grandson Ip-keg-na."

The old man beamed and nodded his head at the group… until his eyes met Eddie's. His eyes widened. "OOKoopik-na!" he cried, pointing.

Richie, exasperated, snapped, "Oh, no, you don't, Pops. We're done with adventures!" To murmurs of assent from the crew, he wrapped his arm around Eddie, and half-ushered, half-shoved him indoors.

Eddie looked back for a final glance at the shaman, who was still staring at him. The old man crouched down to whisper something to the small boy, and the door closed between them.

Chapter 9

Ice Child

Fed, warm, bathed and dry, Eddie and Richie bedded down in twin bunks on opposite sides of a small guest room. Rich, worn out from the day's events, was snoring, but sleep eluded Eddie.

Every time he closed his eyes, his mind skittered across a sequence of terrifying images: himself strapped to the wing of the Viking plane as it screeched down the icy lake throwing up a rooster tail of ice chips… the deck of the Hercules exploding under his feet… standing in the back of the lifeboat as a crew of skeletons swiveled to stare openmouthed at him… opening his mouth to scream but no scream coming out, and then the weight of the massive white bear crushing his chest as its steaming breath and hot drool rolling down his face and…

Something poked his cheek. He gasped desperately and sat up, his heart hammering.

A small boy was standing by his bed – straight black hair, round dark face, dancing dark eyes that reminded Eddie of a playful puppy…

"Hello," the boy said with a smile.

Eddie had no idea who this child was or how he'd gotten into his room. All he could think of to say was, "Um, hello?"

He glanced at Richie, but his friend was still snoring like a chainsaw.

"My name is Ip-keg-na, but everyone calls me Ip," said the boy. "My grandfather says you're the one."

"Um…" said Eddie. "One what?"

"OOkoo-pik-na," Ip said matter-of-factly.

"OO-koo… – what's that?"

Ip, glancing at the sleeping Rich, held his finger to his lips to ask for a whisper. "You're the Ice Child," he said quietly. "That's why I poked you – I wanted to make sure you were real."

"Am I?" Eddie wasn't too sure at that point.

"I don't know," Ip said. "You haven't gone anywhere yet."

If there was one thing Eddie was sure of, that wasn't it. "You could have fooled me. Where else am I supposed to go?"

"Grandfather says you're supposed to go to the far side of the sacred whale burial grounds," the boy said seriously. "It's forbidden for anyone to go there except OOkoo-pik-na." Something in Ip's tone gave Eddie the shivers.

"Well, I hate to disappoint your grandfather," Eddie said firmly. "But I'm here for a different reason."

"What reason?" The boy took a seat on the foot of Eddie's bed, clearly ready for a long conversation.

Eddie glanced over: Rich was still sound asleep. He decided to tell Ip everything. After all, who would understand better than a child? He told Ip about his friendship with Boreas and all the adventures that followed. He even fished in his duffel and got out Boreas's pine cone, which Ip stared at open-mouthed but refused to touch.

"… but I'm afraid Richie's right," Eddie sighed. "I almost got everyone killed twice today."

"I know dreams come at a price, but this is my dream and I don't want anybody else hurt because of me. I guess I need to grow up and just go home to Sonja and Ember."

Ip thought about it, his brow furrowed.

"Maybe not."

"No, Ip. It's just a crazy childhood dream. How many people have almost been killed because of it? It's over."

Ip spoke slowly. "Grandfather told me once about a place marked by a giant totem and a great wall of ice. He said it's on the other side of the burial grounds."

Eddie shrugged. "I've been in a lot of places, and none of them have some magic place that nobody's ever seen and nobody's allowed to go."

"But maybe it's real," the child said earnestly.

"'Maybe' isn't good enough," Eddie grunted. "You're forgetting one thing, Ip – I'm not a child anymore. Thanks, but I think you need to go now. Tell your grandfather he made a mistake."

Ip's face fell. He got up silently and left the room. Eddie closed the door behind him.

Slowly, he sat on his bed, and began wrapping the pinecone back up in tissue paper to kept it safe. Once he'd stowed it in a special pocket of his new duffel bag, he lay down and prepared to get some badly needed sleep.

Just as he was about to close his eyes, he glanced across the room. Rich was awake.

"So, that's the real story," the young captain said.

"Yup." Eddie had no secrets left. "I'm sorry for putting you through this. Let's go home."

"Oh, no you don't!" Rich swung his legs off the bed and sat up, his eyes sparkling with excitement.

"Oh no," Eddie moaned.

"Oh yes," Rich corrected him. "Now that I know the whole story, I actually believe the crazy thing."

Eddie rolled over to face the wall. "Yeah, right."

"No, really. I always wondered why you never froze in the water the day you saved my life. And again, when the Hercules went down. I wouldn't have believed it if I hadn't seen it."

Eddie didn't reply.

"I think the kid may be right," Richie said. "You need to check this totem thing out. You can't quit when you're this close!"

"No?" said Eddie heavily. "Just watch me." He yanked the covers up to his chin.

"Oh, come on," Rich implored. "You've never quit anything in your life."

Clearly, Richie wasn't going to leave him alone until they resolved this. Eddie rolled over with a sigh. "Who am I kidding? My childhood dream almost got everyone killed today."

"Well, yeah," Rich conceded. "Twice. But that's nothing new."

"Hey!" Eddie said indignantly, sitting up and looking annoyed.

"And have you noticed that nobody's ever actually gotten hurt? At least not badly," Rich pointed out. "And think of all the people's lives you've actually made better."

"Hah," Eddie scoffed. "Like who?"

"Me, for one," Rich said. "Without you, I'd never have gotten over my phobia. I wouldn't have taken over my dad's company either. "

"And you'd never have had six or seven nervous breakdowns along the way," Eddie pointed out.

Rich shrugged. "Don't you think I knew what I was signing up for when I chose you as my best friend?"

Eddie's eyes widened. He thought he was dragging a reluctant Richie through his adventures. "Really?"

Rich dropped his usual teasing tone. "Look, Eddie. A lot of people never live their dreams. Or worse, they just let them die. They become empty shell people."

"Empty shell... what?" Eddie's eyebrows creased.

"You know the ones," Rich said. "They're empty. Lifeless and bitter." His features hardened in determination. "And I'm not about to let that happen to you."

Eddie looked down. "But... what if I don't believe anymore?"

"Then you'll have to find a way to start again." Rich made it sound simple. "My dad once told me, just because you got dealt a bad hand doesn't mean you quit. It's how well you play what you've been dealt that makes the difference. That's one reason you're my best friend – because whenever you get dealt a bad hand, you always seem to make something good out of it."

Eddie looked up. "What's the other reason?"

Rich shrugged. "I like crazy people." He grinned his old, teasing smile.

Eddie laughed in spite of himself.

"You're going to follow this thing through, even if I have to carry you there myself." Reaching down, Rich grabbed one of his boots from the floor where he'd kicked it off, reached inside, and pulled out a fat wad of high-denomination bills.

Eddie's mouth hung open.

"I always carry backup cash for emergencies," Rich explained, smiling. "Here." He proffered the money to his friend.

"No, you handle the money," Eddie suggested. "You're the money guy."

Rich looked puzzled. "But I'm not going with you. You heard the kid. You're the Ice Child, remember?"

"But, Richie, I thought you said you'd follow me anywhere." It didn't seem right, following this dream to its end without either his wife-to-be or his best friend by his side.

"Almost anywhere," Rich said. "I'm pretty sure this one you have to do alone."

"Well then," Eddie said, conceding the point. "If not to the North Pole, then how about down the aisle?"

He wouldn't have thought he could startle Richie, but that did it. *"What?!"*

"Sonja and I are getting married," Eddie explained, enjoying the expression of surprise on his friend's face. "Will you be my best man? That is, if she'll still have me."

"Tell you what," Rich said, his eyes dancing. "Go to the ice wall, see the North Wind, find the man in red, say hi, come back in one piece and yeah, I'll be your best man." He shoved the money at Eddie, who took it reluctantly and stashed it in his own boot.

A pause hung in the air.

"There's something I haven't told you yet," Eddie confessed.

Richie raised his eyebrows. "There's *more?!*"

Eddie lunged over and swept up his friend in a bearhug. "I never thanked you for saving my life. Thanks, best friend."

Richie froze for a moment and then returned the hug. "All right, all right already. You know I can't handle the mushy stuff." He dabbed at his eye and shoved his friend away. "Now, let's get some sleep, pal. You're gonna need it. Manny radioed for a ship. It'll be here in the morning, and I want you down at the dock to see us off."

They climbed into their bunks and turned out the light.

Chapter 10

The Shaman

The ship was waiting at the wharf. Eddie was there to say goodbye to his friend. The crew looked puzzled – why would anyone stay here, at the end of the earth? – but Rich, the last to board, wore a satisfied expression.

He put something in Eddie's hand and threw his arms around his friend's neck. "You take care of yourself and come back in one piece," he whispered into Eddie's ear.

"I will," Eddie whispered back.

As they pulled apart, Rich said firmly, "Next time we go somewhere, I'll pick the place. And believe me, it's going to be someplace warm and tropical." He stroded up the gangplank, looking every inch a captain.

Eddie looked at the gift lying in the palm of his hand. It was a set of dog tags on a chain. The inscription read…

IN AN INSANE WORLD

ONLY THE SANE MAN IS CRAZY.

Eddie turned. Richie was smiling down at him from the railing. "Got it, buddy," he said under his breath, and slipped the chain over his head.

He didn't stick around to watch the ship sail, but turned to walk back to the village. Out of the corner of his eye, he saw movement between the cargo crates piled along the dock. He stopped, and out popped Ip.

"What are you doing here?!" Eddie asked, surprised to see the boy again.

"I knew you wouldn't leave." Ip was smiling widely.

Eddie grunted. "Glad I didn't disappoint you." He kept walking.

"Grandfather says you're in danger," Ip chattered, trotting to keep up with Eddie's longer stride.

"Yeah, I get that a lot."

"He wants to see you," the boy said as he bounced along.

"I think I'll pass on the whole OOkoo-whatchamacallit thing, thanks." Eddie paused, an idea striking him. "Tell you what. How about telling me something that can actually help me, like where I can get a snowmobile or a dogsled?"

"Sure!" Ip chirped. "I can do that." Taking his hand, the boy led him into the village.

Eddie noticed Ip's expression was a bit mischievous.

"Where are we going?" Eddie asked.

"To my grandfather," Ip said triumphantly.

Eddie stopped in his tracks. "I thought I told you..."

Ip grinned triumphantly. "He's the only sled builder in the village. He's the village sled-dog trainer too."

Eddie sighed. "I might have known."

At the end of the outpost, a small shack stood. Snowbanks had been built all around it, giving the shack the look of a tiny fortress. Eddie could see smoke streaming out of a tin pipe protruding from the roof. Dogs were barking somewhere nearby.

Ip didn't stop to knock, he just barged in the door. "Ku-ko," he shouted – which Eddie guessed must mean "grandfather."

He followed the boy in. A flurry of snowflakes followed them inside.

As Eddie's eyes gradually adjusted to the dim hazy interior, he could see Ip warming his hands by a large, modern wood stove. The old shaman, Ku-dako, was sitting in a rocker, a section of bridle in his hands and some tools on a nearby table. The old man and the young boy were chattering in Inuktitut. Eddie couldn't understand a word, so he occupied himself by looking around the cabin.

He was surprised to see the tables stacked with high-end electronics. On the walls, handsome Inuit art – apparently the dogsled business paid well. But for all its comforts, the cabin smelled strongly of dogs, animal hide and wood smoke.

Suddenly Eddie noticed that everything had gone quiet. Ip and his grandfather were both staring at him expectantly.

"Um, hi?" he said, raising his hand in an awkward wave.

The old man smiled and motioned him toward a big brown leather chair near the fire. Eddie removed his parka and little Ip ran over and took it from him. Ip hung the parka on a peg by the door along with his own, then plopped cross legged onto the floor between the two men.

"I'm here to rent a dogsled, supplies and a seasoned team of dogs," said Eddie, taking out the wad of cash Rich had given him.

"I know, and I also know you are in danger." replied Ku-dako.

Eddie looked into the old man's eyes, calm and sure – they reminded him of polished onyx. However, the shaman's face was as wrinkled as a dried apple, his long white hair wispy and unkempt. Ku-dako wore a shirt of some sort of soft leather, decorated with interact Inuit artwork.

The old man was speaking. "Have you ever handled a team of dogs, or a sled, before?"

151

"No," Eddie said. "Is that why I'm in danger?"

Ku-dako shook his head. "You are in danger because you have two wolves fighting inside you." He reached for a pipe, tamped some tobacco into the bowl, and lit it.

"Two wolves?" Eddie's brow creased.

Ku-dako exhaled a twin stream of white smoke from his nostrils. "One is OOkoo-pik-na. He has the heart of a child, pure and trusting. His power is to bring dreams into the material world."

"And the other?" Eddie asked, leaning forward.

Ku-dako fussed a little with his pipe. "The other is Noc-plac-ta, whose heart is an empty shell, where dreams once lived. He is trapped in the material world, forever chasing after his lost dreams so he is always angry, always sad."

Eddie dropped back in his chair, stunned at the echo of Richie's words. The shaman, unruffled, continued to enjoy his smoke. Finally, Eddie spoke, "Which one will win?"

Ku-dako leaned back in his rocker and thought. The smoke formed a ghostly cloud around his head.

"Whichever one you feed," he said at length.

"Whoa," marveled little Ip, gaping.

Eddie didn't reply.

Ku-dako sat up straighter. "I will give you a sled and my best dogs, because I know where you must go. You will need only minimum training, because the dogs know the way." He rose from his chair with some effort. From the woodpile by the stove, he drew an iron poker. Using it to open the door of the stove, he threw in a few more sticks, and flames rose. "I would go with you, but powerful magic guards that place. None but OOkoo-pik-na may enter."

"Really, Grandpa? Real magic?" blurted Ip, unable to control himself.

Eddie noticed the old man's hands trembling with age as he closed the stove door, stowed the poker and returned to his chair to speak again, ignoring his grandson for the moment. "You must pass through the ancient whale burial grounds to find what you seek," he said.

Eddie and Ip both leaned forward, mesmerized.

153

"I have only been there once, and I battled a fierce blizzard on the way. I saw the giant totem, and the great wall of ice you seek. I camped there for one night. Something powerful happened as I slept."

"What, Grandpa?" Ip was rapt.

Eddie didn't have to ask: he was pretty sure he already knew the answer.

"The wind spoke to me in a dream," the old man said, looking Eddie straight in the eye.

"What did it say?" Ip could hardly hold still.

"The wind said that someday OOkoo-pik-na might come," Ku-dako replied. "It showed me the vision of the two wolves. It said I would know OOkoo-pik-na by his eyes, blue as the ice fields of the north."

Ip turned to stare open-mouthed at Eddie's blue eyes. "Whoa," he said faintly.

"The wind gave me a warning also," the old man said. "It said, 'The way is shut, none but OOkoo-pik-na may pass. Now go! GO!' And I woke up with a scream. I left that place and never returned."

"Whoa!" Ip marveled. "I gotta see this!"

Both men's heads snapped around. They glared at the excited boy. *"Ip!"*

"What?" Ip said innocently.

Ku-dako took a deep breath, then smiled, his face falling into a million wrinkles. "I will send you… part of the way."

Ip beamed ear to ear.

Eddie looked skeptical.

"He needs a ride back to his mother in the next village," the shaman explained. "The dogs trust him, and he can teach you how to handle the sled along the way."

"Cool! Can we go now?" exclaimed Ip, leaping to his feet and running for his parka.

"Tomorrow," his grandfather said repressively. "Now, go into the sled room and start getting things ready."

"Yes, Ku-Ko!" Ip sprang from the floor and bounced out of the room.

Ku-dako stood, and laid an ancient hand on Eddie's shoulder. "I will take no money," he said. "But I have one request."

"Of course," replied Eddie. "What can I do?"

From a wall, Ku-dako pulled down a great hunting spear, which he placed across Eddie's lap. "There is a debt I must repay. I am too old now, so I must ask you to do it for me. If it is not returned, my spirit must be bound by the debt and never allowed to cross over to the other side." For the first time, the shaman sounded every year of his age.

Eddie looked at the spear. It was an awesome thing, fully seven feet long and straight as an arrow. The base of the spear was fashioned from wood, with carved runes running its length. Red dye had been rubbed into them – they seemed to tell some sort of story, but Eddie had no idea what it was. The back end was pierced with a heavy iron ring that Eddie assumed was for rope. But the business end was the most formidable part: a black iron spearhead, the size of Eddie's hand, fiercely barbed and bound to the wood with leather strapping. Three carved ivory barbs protruded from the top end of the wood above the strapping – Eddie was pretty sure he could see dried blood stains in the carvings.

It was a fearsome weapon. Eddie looked up at Ku-dako a bit uneasily.

"There may come a time when you may need to use it," the old man said solemnly.

"Use it?!" Eddie gasped. "Me? Why? When?"

"A time of testing," the shaman said, laying his hand on Eddie's shoulder.

"The testing of your spirit." He cleared his throat and turned away.

"How will I know what to do?" Eddie's voice sounded confused.

"You'll know," replied Ku-dako. Shuffling toward the hallway, he gestured for Eddie to follow. "Ip-keg-na will help you get safely to the next village. From there, you will need to trust in the dogs and animal guides."

Eddie followed Ku-dako down the hall. "Animal guides?"

"Yes," nodded Ku-dako matter-of-factly. "Animal guides are sent to help you when you need it most. You must always accept the help of an animal guide, and you must always be grateful."

"Um, okay," Eddie said dubiously.

The two men stopped at a door covered by an animal-skin curtain. "Here is a room for you to get some rest," said Ku-dako, holding the curtain open. "You have an early start tomorrow. Ip and I will prepare your sled."

He held out his hand. Eddie put the spear in it.

The old man turned and shuffled down the hallway and into the darkness. His voice floated back, "Dream well, OOkoo-pik-na..."

Chapter 11

Across the Void

The weather was cold and windy the next morning as Ip and Eddie hit the trail but they had toasty mukluks to protect them against the harsh elements. Kudako was right. Ip knew the team of dogs very well and was a talented teacher. The two laughed and joked as they sledded. Eddie found himself growing very attached to the bright little boy. Ip reminded him of himself as a child, the self he had feared he'd lost.

They traveled for nearly a week before reaching Ip's mother's village. Saying goodbye wasn't easy, Ip sulked and even cried a tear or two. He desperately wanted to join Eddie for the rest of the trip.

Eddie felt a little like crying himself. "You know I have to do this part alone," he said to the unhappy boy. "Remember what your grandfather said – only OOkoo-pik-na can go, and it's the only way to make sure the right wolf wins."

Ip bit his lip and glowered. "I can help. You're not that good with the sled yet, and you know it."

Eddie didn't reply because he knew Ip was right. He turned away to help load the sled.

Ip tugged the back of his coat. "Grownups are pretty dumb, but you're the dumbest one yet. You let all your friends help you but when you need it the most, you won't let me! It's because I'm a kid, isn't it?"

Eddie swallowed hard.

"Why can't you believe in me?" Ip cried.

The words stuck like a knife into Eddie's heart. He remembered wanting the same thing all his life. His eyes welled up. He crouched down to Ip's level and put his hands on the child's shoulders.

"I'd love to take you, but your grandfather said no."

A fat tear rolled down Ip's cheek. He dashed it away with his coat sleeve.

Eddie started to stand, but before he could straighten his legs, Ip had thrown his arms around Eddie's neck in a desperate hug.

Eddie felt his heart crack. "I'll be back, Ip. I promise." Then he broke the tension with a smile. "If I don't get the dogs and sled back to your grandpa in good condition, I'll never hear the end of it."

Ip wasn't interested in being joked with. He frowned. "If I can't go with you, at least take this." He pulled a knife from somewhere within his coat and handed it, handle-first, to Eddie. "It's my lucky knife. I made it myself."

Eddie looked at the tool in his hand. While it was clearly the work of a child, a lot of care had gone into its making: it was clean and functional, protected by an animal-skin sheath with a belt loop. Eddie didn't want to take something that was so precious to its owner, but Ip was gazing at him solemnly and he didn't dare refuse.

"Thank you, Ip." Eddie strapped the tool onto his belt. Ip went to say goodbye to the dogs.

Eddie turned to get one last set of directions from a villager.

Only a few were there to see him off because they knew he was headed to the forbidden burial grounds. By the time he turned back, Ip was gone.

Fighting a lonely pang, Eddie shrugged. "Guess he didn't want to stick around." He mounted the sled, called "Mush," and was off into the great white void of endless night.

By the end of the first hour, he had never felt so alone. He and the dogs were the only life as far as the eye could. A small spec under a starlit sky across the vast expanse of white. The only sounds were the swish of the sled runners, the panting of the dogs, and the light jingle of the bridles. The natural beauty of the untamed vastness took his breath away and he shivered.

He passed the time watching the snow dance across the surface of the featureless dark landscape. The stars above were mirrored by the sparkle of snowflakes in the endless expanse.

After a full day of travel, Eddie stopped to get some sleep. As he leaned back against his bedroll, a shower of shooting stars lit up the night sky above him. He marveled at their beauty.

The dogs whined and he tore himself reluctantly away from the spectacle. The poor things must be hungry! He chided himself for losing track of the time and climbed to his feet to find something for them to eat. He walked over to the dog sled and untied the straps. Eddie lifted the flap covering the supplies on the back of the sled. None of the packages were labeled and he couldn't remember which one contained seal meat for the dogs.

"Where is that damn meat?" he grumbled to himself as he rummaged through the supplies.

A familiar-looking package appeared under his nose.

"Thanks," he said automatically as he noticed the small mittened hand holding it out.

He accepted it and turned to give it to the dogs then did a double take. "What the?..."

Ip's grinning face was peering out from under the flap.

"Ip! Are you crazy?!" Eddie shouted in exasperation.

"You're a fine one to talk," Ip pointed out as he came out of his hiding place.

"Now you *have* to take me, you're too far out to turn around."

Eddie started to argue, then shook his head helplessly. "Your grandfather is going to kill me."

"Yup," Ip grinned. "But not until we're back."

Chapter 12

Dark Places

Near the end of the following day, a mountain range appeared on the horizon. As they grew closer, a full moon peeked over it. The terrain grew rough, making the sled bounce and jerk as it ran.

"Whoa!" shouted Ip, and the dogs skidded to a halt. A huge crater yawned before them.

"Can we go around?" Eddie asked.

Ip scanned the width of the crater with his expert eye. "No, it's too wide. It'd be a day or two more if we did." The moon lit the great basin, but its light was too dim to so see the terrain within. A light mist was wafting up from the crater's depths and creeping over its edges. The boy shook his head. "Never seen anything like this before. Looks kind of strange to me."

"Do we have a choice?" Eddie pointed out.

Ip shrugged. "Guess not."

"Then let's go for it."

Ip mushed the dogs. They started forward and crossed the outer lip. As they began to descend, an odd darkness began to surround them.

Ip stopped the sled again. "Something's wrong. This darkness isn't right."

Eddie nodded. "Yeah, I can feel it too." He looked around.

Ip yelped and elbowed him. "Look!" The boy pointed upward. The edge of the moon was clipped away.

"Oh," Eddie said, relieved. "Just a lunar eclipse."

Ip looked unhappy. "My grandfather would say this is a very bad sign."

Eddie shrugged. "Like you said, no choice."

Ip hesitated, then picked up the reins again. As they descended into the crater, they saw large buckled sections of ice rearing up on either side of them. In the distance, other strange shapes appeared out of the ice. It looked to Eddie like a forest of frozen tree trunks.

They kept going.

"Oh, gosh," gasped Ip, yanking on the reins.

As they pulled up to the strange formations, they could see more clearly: the sled stood on the border of a gigantic sea of bones.

The dogs came to a halt, whimpering. Eddie felt the hair standing on the back of his neck. An eery mist drifted around the frozen monoliths...

Ip whispered, "Maybe this wasn't such a good idea. I'm scared."

Eddie put a hand on his shoulder. "Me, too."

Ip looked up at him reproachfully. "Some help *you* are."

"Well, I didn't want you to feel alone."

Ip shook his head. Taking a deep breath, he climbed from the sled and grasped the lead dog's bridle. Silently, he walked into the fossilized forest, the sled inching along behind him.

Nobody made a sound as they drifted through the misty graveyard. The ghoulish bones made a kind of maze, and it was taking all Ip's skill to keep the dogs and sled from getting tangled or damaged.

As if that weren't enough, the ice was making strange creaking noises, as though the place were awake and voicing its ghostly protests about their intrusion.

Eddie's stomach twisted as he thought about the results of getting lost in the maze, or the sled getting damaged, or one of the dogs, out here beyond where anyone could help them. He didn't mention his worries to Ip, but he was pretty sure the boy was thinking the same thing.

The dogs' ears were back and their tails tucked between their legs. Ip walked on, slowly but steadily.

Eddie could hear his own breath. "Did you see that? Off to the left." he whispered at Ip.

Ip looked all around, his eyes wide.

"No" he hissed. "Stop freaking me out!"

Suddenly a crack sounded to their left. Eddie jumped and gasped. The dogs whined. As they watched, a chunk of snow toppled form one of the tall rib bones and fell with a thud.

"Okay, that does it, we're out of here," Ip stated.

He leapt back onto the sled and cracked the reins over the dogs' backs. The dogs didn't need any urging – they took off fast, and the sled leapt over the snow.

Something else leapt behind them. Eddie looked back and his mouth fell open in horror. "IP! BEAR!!" he shouted.

Ip looked behind him, his eyes widening in terror as he took in the enormous polar bear chasing them. The dogs caught the predator's scent and stretched into a full terrified sprint.

Eddie knew this bear. There was a black, charred mark in the fur of its right shoulder. When it opened its mouth, he saw the broken front tooth.

The dogs were exhausted and the bear was gaining on them. Thinking fast, Eddie freed the handmade knife Ip had given him from its sheath and cut the straps holding their packs to the sled. Their supplies scattered all over the snow and the lightened sled sped out of the crater. The bear snarled in frustration as they flew safely away.

Eddie giggled in hysterical relief but his voice was drowned by the pistol-shot sound of a crack in the ice.

A gaping fissure began to open to their right. The ice all around them began to shake and smaller cracks formed everywhere. The dogs, unbelievably, ran even faster, but the ground was giving way all around them. Their supplies tumbled to the bottom of the expanding chasm which opened behind them.

A rush of snow blew up into Eddie's face as he felt the world dip under their runners. Ip went flying to one side, the reins still clutched in his sturdy little hands.

Eddie tried to scream, but the wind ripped the sound from his mouth. All he could do was close his eyes, hang on to the sled.

Chapter 13

The Two Wolves

They cleared the crevasse by inches. Ip pulled desperately at the reins and the exhausted dogs dropped to the ground panting.

Ip looked back with his mouth hanging open. "All the supplies are gone!"

"It was the best I could do, considering the situation," Eddie rasped, still too exhausted to rise from the snow.

"Great," Ip snapped.

"Well, I figured anything that got us out of there was a good idea."

Ip looked like he wanted to argue, but there really wasn't much to say. Then he did a double take. "Look!"

They weren't the only ones caught by the collapse. The giant polar bear was trapped on a ledge jutting from the opposite side of the crevasse. He clawed at the walls, moaning, trying to get away.

"Hah!" Eddie yelled triumphantly at the stranded bear. "Serves you right!"

"Hey," Ip protested. "That's not funny."

Eddie wasn't feeling all that sympathetic.

"What do you mean? That bear tried to eat us "

Bears eat meat, we're meat," Ip shrugged. "And look, that ledge is too low – he's trapped. Don't you think that's a horrible way to die?"

When Eddie stopped to think about it, Ip was right. Eddie looked down at the sled and noticed that Kudako's fearsome spear was still strapped to its side. He bent down to untie it.

"What are you doing?" Ip asked nervously.

"Better to kill him quickly than let him die of thirst and starvation," Eddie replied.

Ip's eyes widened. "I didn't mean for you to kill him. We only kill to eat. This isn't right."

"Ip, this isn't for sport. It's a mercy killing."

Ip held his ground, crossing his arms and scowling.

This was no time to argue. "Ip, go to the front of the sled and tend to the dogs."

"But…"

"Now. I mean it." Eddie's tone brooked no argument.

Ip gave Eddie a killing glare, then turned, muttering "Assassin!" under his breath as he stomped over to the dogs.

Eddie raised the great spear to his shoulder and took careful aim. The half-light of the eclipse made aiming difficult. The bear had stopped clawing at the wall and looked into Eddie's eyes, clearly understanding his fate.

The two figures silently stared at each other for a long moment.

"I only have one shot," Eddie muttered to himself. Taking a deep breath, he threw the spear with all his strength.

The spear hissed as it cut through the frosty air. Eddie closed his eyes and listened for the spear hit its target.

He heard a solid "Thud" as the spear met its mark.

He opened his eyes…

"Yes!" he shouted in triumph. The great spear was buried halfway up the wall. Using it like the rung of a ladder, the bear climbed free.

"Hey, I thought you were going to kill him!" questioned Ip as he ran up to the edge.

"I was," Eddie explained. "But then I realized that he'd actually saved our lives. He was trying to chase us away from the breaking ice. I think he was one of the animal guides your grandfather told me about."

"Whoa." Ip's eyes were like saucers. "Maybe the good wolf inside you *has* won!"

"I hope so, Ip," Eddie said. He picked Ip up and plopped him back in the sled, climbing on behind him. "I really hope so."

"In that case…" Ip fished around in his pockets and pulled out a small, battered pinecone. "I found this in Grandpa's guest room after you left. You must have forgotten it. I knew it was important, so I brought it for you. A grownup wouldn't care, but OOkoo-pik-nah would."

"Oh, my gosh." Eddie blinked back tears: he'd thought Boreas's gift was gone with all the rest of their supplies. "Ip, you are a marvel." He hugged the boy, overcome with gratitude.

"I get that a lot," Ip grinned, then shook the reins and called "Mush!"

As the dogs began to pull, Eddie looked back over his shoulder. Just for a moment, he thought he saw the giant bear and the shaman staring back at him from the other edge of the crevasse. Suddenly, a shower of snow stung his face, and when he looked back again, they were gone.

He grinned and shook his head. "Naaah," he said under his breath.

As they continued, the air grew darker as the eclipse approached its totality. The wind was picking up and the dogs had gotten their second wind. Ip shouted with excitement as they neared the mountain range that lie just ahead.

Eddie felt a moment of déjà vu: the place looked just like Boreas had shown him, all those years ago. "Ip, I think this is it!" he shouted excitedly.

"What?" Ip said, cupping his hand over his ear. It was only then that Eddie noticed a soft rumble, growing louder by the second. He turned around to see what it was and gasped at the sight.

A towering wave of wind and snow was bearing down on them. It stretched from one horizon to the other.

"MUSH!" shrieked Ip.

The dogs leaped forward in search of cover. However, they couldn't outrun the blizzard. It crashed down upon them, whiting out their vision.

Eddie felt the sled jolt underneath him. It heaved into the air as it hit a buckle in the ice. He lost his grip and tumbled clear. The sled instantly disappeared into the storm. He shouted, but the fierce roar of the blizzard was deafening.

Eddie wandered aimlessly through the sea of white, calling for Ip and the dogs. He heard nothing but the blizzard's wail.

Eventually he found an ice shelf to hide under and waited for the storm to pass.

As Eddie sat safely under the ice shelf, he worried about Ip and the dogs.

"I must find them!" he thought as he impatiently waited.

After a while the storm lulled him into a deep sleep.

Chapter 14

Magic and Ice

When Eddie awoke is was eerily quiet. The storm had passed, and the snow sparkled on the ground like diamonds. The moon was in full eclipse, giving the terrain a ghostly deep purple color.

"I'm sure this would be another of the old man's bad omens," Eddie thought.

Turning to survey his position, Eddie gasped: a gigantic wall of ice filled his vision, gleaming mirror-like, stretching from one horizon to the other.

A few hundred yards away stood a tall totem pole, carved from top to bottom with runes he couldn't decipher at that distance.

"I made it," Eddie breathed.

But he'd made it without Ip. His shoulders slumped. He looked around, sharpening his ears, hoping to catch his young friend's call or the bark of one of the dogs. Ignoring the totem and the wall, Eddie began walking, shouting "Ip! Ip!"as loud as he could. He walked for a long time, calling until his voice was hoarse.

Suddenly he stopped. "What am I doing? My best chance is back at the wall." He turned and ran, following his footprints. He ran past the huge totem, which looked like a monolith half buried in the ice. Its emblems, faces, animals and mythical creatures, looked down on him silently as he ran by.

When he finally stopped to catch his breath, he looked up. The wall was so tall beside him that he couldn't see the top. Wonderingly, he reached out one mittened hand and touched its glossy surface, peering into its translucent purple and blue depths.

What if it doesn't open? he thought. What if he'd imagined everything Boreas had told him so long ago?

He exhaled heavily, doing his best to push such thoughts from his head. "If I keep thinking like this, it *definitely* won't open."

Eddie reached down and gently gathered a handful of snow, it sparkled like stardust in his mitten.

Gazing up into the clear night, he hesitated. The stars winked down at him, offering a spark of hope.

"I guess this is it," he said, and took a deep breath. Eddie threw the snow high into the air, and yelled the magic word as loudly as he could.

"MORIAH!!!"

Her name echoed off the canyon walls, and faded away. The snow fell softly to his feet and there was silence. Nothing happened.

Eddie waited and waited.

"Oh, no," he moaned. His legs gave way and he fell to his knees. With his head bowed, he knelt in the snow, his shoulders slumped in defeat. Tears streamed down his cheeks.

He felt his heart breaking with the realization of all that he'd lost.

Ip and the dogs were gone. He'd never see Andrew, Richie, Sonya or Ember again.

He just couldn't understand it.

How could Boreas never have existed? Here he was, right in front of the wall of ice, it had to be real.

However, he had no way to escape this frozen wasteland. Eddie had never felt so alone, so empty.

As his last tear fell, it turned to ice, and landed softly on the snow.

Chapter 15

Lost and Found

To Eddie, moments felt like hours as he knelt there, feeling his life crumble. It finally ended when he heard a gentle jingle behind him.

He turned and cried out in disbelief. It was Ip and the dogs! He ran to greet them.

"Whoa," Ip cried, grinning all over.

Eddie hugged the little boy tightly to him. "I've been looking all over for you. I was so worried!"

Ip looked up at Eddie like he was crazy. "Worried about *me?* I'm not the one stranded in the middle of nowhere without a sled. I'm here to save *you.*"

Eddie laughed.

"Right you are Ip."

But then, Ip gasped as he noticed the giant totem pole. "So, this is it," he said.

Eddie nodded, his face falling.

"Well, what are you waiting for? Open it!" Ip urged.

"I already tried. It didn't work." Eddie looked away.

"You must have missed something," reasoned Ip. "What does the magic word mean, anyway?"

"It doesn't mean anything," Eddie said. "It's just the name of the South Wind."

"Ah, that's different," Ip said, his brow clearing. "Did you just yell at her? Or did you call to her? You know, like you'd call to an old friend?"

Eddie's mouth fell open. "Ip, you're a genius!" he crowed, grabbing the boy by his shoulders and shaking him.

Ip grinned. "Yeah, I get that a lot."

Smiling, Eddie ran back to the spot he'd tried before. He picked up another handful of snow. This time, as he tossed it into the air, he reached deep into his heart, saying the name as if he were speaking to a beloved old friend: "MORIAH!"

And they waited. Once again, the voice echoed off the wall, and faded into the snow.

The eclipse had broken and a slim crescent of white light beamed from its edge.

In the distance, Eddie heard a sound: the high, pure tone of a woman, singing. As he looked out, he noticed a soft breeze drifted over the surface of the snow.

Ip's eyes were huge. "Did you hear that?"

Eddie stood motionless as he heard the tinkling of wind chimes. The gentle breeze made the shimmering snowflakes dance around his feet. Suddenly, they sped up the ice wall like a silver wave.

The darkness came to life as the Northern Lights danced across the sky in waves of color. The light caught the whirling snow and filled the air with sparkles of color.

The magic gate appeared as a glowing outline in the ice. Eddie and Ip stood transfixed, staring, at the most beautiful thing they had ever seen.

Until they saw Moriah.

She appeared before them, breathtakingly beautiful in a swirling vortex of glittering snow. Her long hair flowed white down her back and a simmering silver gown billowed around her. She motioned with her slim white hands and the glowing lines of the gate began to separate. The ice popped and cracked in release as the gate opened. Mist poured out, as the doors came to rest.

Breathlessly, they stepped forward. The open gates revealed a great hall of arches, its ice pillars emitting soft blue light.

Ip stopped and stood agape at the splendor.

"Whaddaya think, buddy?" said Eddie. "Did I call it?"

"Whoa," Ip said simply.

"There's more," Eddie told him, picking him up and swinging him into the sled. "Are you ready to see the most magical thing in the world?"

"I thought I just did," Ip said, his head swiveling to take it all in.

"Not even close," Eddie assured him. "Let's go."

They mushed the dogs inside. As they passed Moriah, Eddie bowed his head in thanks. The lovely South Wind smiled and waved them through.

They emerged from the hall of pillars and were greeted by a cheering crowd of elves.

"Check it out!" Ip grinned. "Everyone's my size! I think I'm going to like this place!"

"I'm pretty sure you will," Eddie grinned.

All the elves thronged around the sled as it came to a stop. "I'm here to see the man in charge," Eddie announced.

"Right away, sir." A cheerful elf replied.

"Ip, I need you to stay with the sled. I'm sure the elves will take care of the dogs and get us set up with supplies for the trip back."

"If I say yes, will you bring Santa down to meet me?" Ip bartered.

Eddie grinned. "You drive a hard bargain. I'll see what I can do." He patted his young friend on the shoulder, and turned to go.

An honor guard of elves escorted Eddie to the castle. The village was unbelievably lovely. It was just as the North Wind had shown him, so many years before.

When Eddie arrived at the castle, the head elf took him by the hand and led him to the door of Santa's office. The elf stopped and let Eddie enter.

A solitary figure, dressed in red, was seated at a large, ornate desk at the far end of the room. He had his head down and was concentrating on marking a long sheet of paper before him. A smoldering pipe stood in a stand near his hand, its smoke forming shapes – a rocking horse, a jack-in-the-box, a teddy bear – as it rose to the ceiling.

The figure in red did not raise his head, but continued to make check marks. The long sheet of paper slid along the desk as he worked, rolling in coils across the floor.

"Well, young man, I'm very happy to see that you made it," the man in red said without looking up.

"You know who I am?" asked Eddie.

The man looked up at last. He had rosy cheeks, a fluffy white beard, and cheerful blue eyes behind little wire-framed spectacles.

"Of course I do," Santa said. "I know who everyone is. I know everything about you. I know about your friendship with the North Wind. I even saw the moment when you began to doubt yourself." He picked up his pipe and took a contented puff.

"Then why didn't you help me?" asked Eddie.

Santa blew a stream of smoke into the room. It smelled of cinnamon and oranges. "My boy, I couldn't help you. Only you could find the child within your heart. And only someone who has found the child within their heart can come here." He looked calmly around the big room, whose shelves were piled high with toys, books, gadgets and ledgers.

Eddie was speechless.

Santa took off his reading glasses and put them on his desk. "I know it wasn't easy. But I was rooting for you. And you made it." He smiled widely and stood. "Now, I believe we have some business to take care of."

"So you'll help?" breathed Eddie, hardly daring to believe it.

Santa walked over and put his hand on Eddie's shoulder. "I believe you have an old friend you've been wanting to see. Let's not keep him waiting."

Eddie followed Santa down a long hallway.

Open doors on either side showed elves at work: hammering bits of wood, sewing dolls and stuffed toys, tinkering with electronic gadgets, baking gingerbread.

"I believe it's a good idea to bring a gift when going to visit someone," noted Santa, as they rounded a corner and entered what appeared to be a barn door.

Eddie gasped: a beautifully decorated sleigh stood before them, with a full team of reindeer pawing and snorting. Awestruck, he stopped and stared.

"Come on, lad," Santa said with a trace of impatience, and climbed into the sleigh.

Eddie shook his head as if to wake himself. "They're never going to believe this." He climbed aboard. "I'm not sure if *I* believe this."

Santa chuckled. "That's better. So, have you chosen your gift?"

Eddie looked blank.

"Come on, lad," the red-suited gentleman urged. "Close your eyes and think of something from your past. Something from your heart."

Eddie closed his eyes. A scene sprang up: a child's mitted hand, with a pine cone resting in it… and Boreas's voice:

"While all the other plants sleep under the snow, the pine tree lives… The rest of the world hides away when the north wind comes to call. Only the pine tree greets me with life and happiness."

Eddie heard his own child-voice. *"And me,"* it said. *"I do, too."*

And the North Wind's chuckle: ***"And you, Eddie."***

Eddie's eyes flew open. "A pinecone!" He reached into his pocket and pulled out the very pinecone that Boreas had given him, all those long years ago.

Santa looked at the small, battered pinecone that lay in Eddie's palm, and chuckled. "I knew you could do it. Let's go!" The reindeer leaped into the air.

The sleigh soared through jagged mountain tops until Eddie saw a lone spire haloed by a frost cloud. As they drew closer, he saw the mouth of the North Wind's cave. Santa effortlessly brought the sleigh to rest nearby. "It's up to you now."

"But what if he doesn't remember me?"

"The wonderful thing about true friendship is, it's timeless," Santa said with a smile.

Taking a deep breath, Eddie climbed from the sleigh and toward the entrance. The cave before him had long, sharp, icicles hanging from its lip. It was too dark inside to see anything which didn't help.

He turned to look at Santa for reassurance. Santa smiled and made a shooing motion with his red-mittened hand.

Taking a deep breath, Eddie tightened his grip around the pinecone and stepped inside.

Chapter 16

Unexpected Company

Eddie felt very small as he walked inside the enormous cave. An eerie blue glow shone through small cracks in the walls. It was hard to see because the air was thick mist. Ice crystals floated silently all around him and Eddie began to worry.

"What if Boreas doesn't remember me?" he thought.

Suddenly he was nearly blown off his feet by a blast of wind so cold he thought he would freeze into a block of ice.

"WHO DARES ENTER MY CAVE?" The rumbling voice was so deep that it felt like it was shaking his very bones. Eddie faltered. "It… It… It's me, Eddie. You knew as a boy. I've come back as a man."

The familiar face formed out of the fog, huge and stern.

"How can this be? I thought you had forgotten me, as all children do."

"How could I ever forget you? You're my friend!" Eddie pointed out. He held out his hand with the little pinecone in his palm. "Remember? You told me you admired these. You said that pine trees were the only thing that greeted you with life and happiness."

Boreas's foggy eyebrows rose. *"I remember, young Eddie,"* the North Wind rumbled. *"The pine trees, and you."*

"I just went away for a while," Eddie explained. "I went to see all the wonderful places you showed me as a child." He paused. "I never thought this would be one of them." He finished with a smirk.

Boreas's mighty laugh shook the walls. Eddie grinned with pleasure at seeing his friend's happiness.

"You came a long way just to bring me this gift," Boreas boomed. *"Is that the only reason you came?"*

"Well, actually, I wanted to ask for your help," Eddie admitted. He told Boreas the whole story: Richie, Sonya, Ember, Ku-dako, Ip – all the people he'd come to care about in his travels. And he told Boreas about his promise to Andrew, the boy who was so much like Eddie as a child, the boy who loved snow.

The North Wind thought for a few minutes, as the cold frosty air billowed. Finally, he said, *"Place your gift on the floor and step back."*

Eddie obeyed. As he watched, Boreas pursed his great lips as he blew a whispering breath that sounded like the tinkle of icicles falling. The pinecone suddenly glistened with a fine coating of ice crystals that made it shimmer in the pale blue light.

"This cone is now enchanted," the Wind explained. *"If you place it on a windowsill, it will summon the winter snows."*

"Wow," Eddie grinned. "Wait till I tell Andrew!"

"But the boy must remember to take it down by the end of winter. All the seasons need their turn in the cycle of life."

"I promise," said Eddie. "And thank you!"

He bent down to retrieve the sparkling cone. The moment his hand touched it, he felt himself shrinking. He looked down in amazement to find himself a child again.

He looked up at the North Wind, puzzled.

"As you are in your heart, so you will be, for a short while," said Boreas. *"My gift to you."*

Eddie grinned, happy in the way that only a carefree child can be. "Till next time, then!" Then he scampered away, just as he had done as a child after his long talks with Boreas.

Santa's eyebrows rose almost to his white hairline when child-Eddie emerged from the cave. "Why, bless my beard! You're quite a sight," he chuckled.

Eddie bounced into his seat. "Ready!" he cried.

Santa flicked the reins as he looked over at Eddie. "Should I ask?"

Eddie just shook his head, smiling.

During that ride, Eddie remembered how many times as a boy he'd dreamed of this moment, riding through the winter sky alongside Santa Claus. He was so excited he could barely breathe.

By the time they got back to the castle, Eddie was back in his adult body. He looked at Santa in surprise.

"That's better," Santa smiled. "You were a wonderful child, but the world needs grown-up Eddie now."

Eddie nodded and began to climb out of the sleigh – then hesitated. "Oh, I almost forgot!" He reached into his coat pocket and pulled out Ember's letter.

Santa opened it and his sparkling blue eyes ran down the contents. He looked at Eddie. "Sorry, son," he said seriously. "This one's for you."

He handed it over. Eddie looked at it.

DEAR SANTA,

ALL I WANT FOR CHRISTMAS IS MY DADDY.

LOVE

EMBER

Tears sprang to his eyes. Santa put a gentle hand on his shoulder. "I believe it's time you were getting back, don't you think?"

Eddie nodded. "Yes, it is."

"But there's just one more thing…"

Chapter 17

A Time for Goodbyes

Ip, his back turned, was fussing with the bridles on a sled loaded with fresh supplies. The dogs were rested and ready, ears perked and tails waging.

"Why, hello there, young man," Santa said jovially.

Ip turned around. His mouth popped open and his eyes went huge. "WHOA!"

Eddie put a finger under the boy's chin and gently closed his mouth. "Aren't you going to say hello to Mr. Claus, Ip?"

Ip ignored him and ran straight into Santa's waiting arms. Santa smiled and crouched down so that he was at Ip's level. "Think you can get Eddie back safely?" he asked.

"No problem," Ip assured him.

"Good lad," Santa said, and started to stand.

Ip tugged at the red coat. As Santa looked down, he pulled a letter out of his sleeve.

When Eddie looked at him curiously, Ip shrugged. "Just thought I'd cover all the bases."

Santa chuckled. "And so you have." Tucking the letter into a pocket for later reading, he turned to the man and boy. "Now, off with the two of you, while there's time."

The two mounted the sled, directing the dogs toward the gate. "Do you think you'll ever come back?" Ip asked curiously, as the sled began to gather speed.

Eddie thought about it. "Maybe some places, you're only meant to visit once."

He looked back over his shoulder at the castle receding toward the horizon.

"Maybe."

"Grownups," Ip sighed, shaking his head.

The gate closed behind them. As Eddie looked back, the opening disappeared, leaving only the sheer wall of ice behind them.

Ip shook the reins and the dogs settled into a steady trot. "So… what did you get?" the boy asked.

"Who says I got anything?"

There was no fooling Ip. "C'mon, you went to see Santa," the boy pointed out. "What is it?"

Eddie pulled the pinecone from his jacket. Ip looked disappointed. "Isn't that the same pinecone I kept for you?"

"Take another look," Eddie told him. Ip looked and his eyes widened as he saw the glistening surface. "It's magical."

"What's it do?" Ip asked excitedly.

"Well, it summons the winter snows," Eddie explained happily.

Ip looked disgusted. "All this for something that brings *more* snow? Are you crazy? *Grownups!*" he grunted, shaking his head.

Eddie laughed as he put the cone back into his jacket.

"I would've asked for something *really* cool, like a set of magic flying boots," Ip grumbled.

Eddie laughed as the two sped off toward the horizon.

Chapter 18

Last-Minute Arrivals

Eddie reached into his pocket to reassure himself that the ticket to Pittsfield was still there. He could hear the rumbling engine of the last train arriving. He hit the "send" button on a text message – MOM – I'M ON MY WAY – SHOULD BE THERE JUST IN TIME – and ran to make his train.

As he entered his compartment, he plopped down by the window, pulled the enchanted pinecone from his bag and placed it on the windowsill. Soothed by the rhythmic clacking of the train tracks, he drifted into a deep sleep.

The conductor nudged him awake – "Next stop Pittsfield!" He grabbed his things and hurried for the door. On the platform, two smiling faces beamed up at him. He smiled at Andrew.

"It's snowing – just in time for Christmas." Eddie pointed out.

The ground was blanketed in white, and flakes drifted through the air all around them.

"Yeah," grinned Andrew. "It started just an hour or two ago."

"Looks like I kept my promise, then... Oof!" cried Eddie, as his nephew's bearhug almost smothered him.

He looked over at his mother, who was smiling happily at her son and grandson. They went home to get ready for Christmas Eve.

An hour later, the family was gathered around the brightly lit tree. A fire crackled on the hearth.

There was a knock at the front door. Eddie went to answer it.

"Well, aren't you going to let us in, love?" He caught his breath at the familiar voice.

"DADDY!" cried Ember, and sprang into his arms. "Daddy, you gave Santa my letter!"

He looked at Sonya, who smiled and explained, "There was a red envelope under the tree. When I picked it up, it brought us here."

"I love you, Daddy!" Ember squealed, throwing her arms around his neck.

Everybody gathered around the front door to see what was causing the commotion. Eddie beamed as he showed Sonya and Ember in. "Mom, can we make two more places for dinner?"

His mom's eyes were wide. "Of course," she said, and bustled off to make room.

Later that evening the children gathered by the fire with their beloved uncle. Eddie and Sonya told stories about their adventures. Then he told them of his visit to the North Wind's home. After he had finished, he gave Andrew the magical pine cone. Andrew held it for all of the children to see. Its frosty edges sparkled in the fire light. Andrew eagerly agreed to keep his promise to the North Wind. Eddie smiled, his lap full of his sleepy daughter.

Later that night Eddie found the boy fast asleep, the magic pine cone lovingly placed on the sill by his bed. Looking through the frosty glass, he watched snow softly falling.

To this day pinecones are given on Christmas Eve as gifts of love and friendship, reminding us that magic will always be with us if we keep love in our hearts.

Epilogue

Meanwhile, a thousands of miles away...

Ip's eyes went wide as he pulled the wrappings from a box. "Whoa!" he cried. Moments later, he was soaring like a bird across the Arctic vista, borne up by his shiny-new Christmas boots.

THE END

Recognition and Appreciations

This story began as most stories do, from an afternoon of storytelling one Christmas. I was amazed at the reaction I received from the children. However, I was busy with other projects. Just the same, kept the story in the back of my mind because of the profound impact it made. Some years later I wrote the original story which is a children's picture book and the companion to this novel. Oddly, the novel was never a vision of mine. As I came across professional artists, animators and even screen play writers, I was strongly encouraged to create the version before you. Though many times the story had simply fallen to the wayside, it seemed to have a life of its own and kept getting interest from unexpected places.

Here are some people and institutions I would like to offer my gratitude.

To the San Francisco Endeavor Foundation for the Arts, who helped make this book a reality.
Emma J Wright, the cover illustrator.

My editor, Janet Harding from the Active Voice who provided her expertise and offered some delightful lightheartedness to these pages.

To City of Pittsfield, for offering the perfect setting for magic and storytelling.

Cafe Namaste, Pittsfield MA - A cozy little nook who promoted my book in the early days.

Most importantly, to my spouse Mike Arnold, for his unwavering support from a simple story line to its final published version. I will always be grateful for his belief in the story which refused to die.

May it live on in the hearts of all who read it.

www.ingramcontent.com/pod-product-compliance
Lightning Source LLC
Chambersburg PA
CBHW070818120626
46556CB00002B/555